BEST OF *Friends*

Peter A Stankovic

Ordering Information:

Prime Seven Media
518 Landmann St.
Tomah City, WI 54660

Printed in the United States of America

Other novels by Peter A Stankovic

LACK OF AMBITION

CHEATERS

CROOKS AND LOSERS

STRANGER

THE LOST HOURS

MAIL ORDER BRIDE

THE HEIRS

MURDER IN CHATSWOOD

THE WOMAN WHO ALWAYS WORE BLACK

THE BIGAMIST

This book is dedicated to:

Alexander Stankovic
Michael Stankovic
Harry Stankovic

ONE

Saturday

I KNEW IT WAS MURDER as soon as I saw the knife sticking out of his neck. I'm a homicide detective and I've seen many grisly things, but it never gets easy to take. The amount of blood all over the floor of the hotel cabin is something else. Seems like the entire floor is engulfed in this red liquid. Using my gloves, I check the body for a wallet or phone. Nothing. Then I tiptoe around the mess and search the drawers on the bedside table. I ruffle through papers and see some coins spread around but underneath a wad of bills, I find a wallet with a four twenty dollar and two fifty-dollar notes but there is no phone. It doesn't appear to be robbery. I place the wallet into an evidence bag. It appears that the guy was in here by himself as I can't see any signs of women's clothing or cosmetics.

Two uniformed officers, from the local Katoomba station, arrived first, I've been told, and they contacted the Forensic Services, members of whom are gathered about doing their jobs. I nod hello to Samuel Ho, a guy with whom I've been to other crime scenes. He nods back, like me, not given to wild expressions of acknowledgement.

I check my iPhone watch which records steps, heart rate and other things. It also shows the time which, at the moment, reveals a digital time of 7:18 a.m. Bloody early. I haven't even had time for my coffee. I was contacted by somebody at five o'clock in my apartment in Collaroy. I can't even remember who the hell called. Why me? Surely there was a detective living closer to the Blue Mountains. Still,

I got dressed and drove to Katoomba in good time, the traffic being light at this time of day on a Saturday.

"Time of death?' I ask.

'We'll know for sure in due course, but I'd guess between two o'clock and three o'clock this morning,' says Ho.

'Who found him and what time was that?'

'A couple of guests. The cabin, as you can see, is outside the swimming pool. The man and his girlfriend were wandering around and saw the light on. They said they went to explore and found the door ajar. When they pushed it open, they saw the man and the blood.'

'Time?'

'Around three, I think.'

'Do we have their names?'

'See the uniforms. They took notes.'

'Thanks mate,' I say, trudging outside. The swimming pool is only a few metres away. I walk up to where the uniformed officers are standing at the far end of the pool. Before I can speak with them, a woman hurries along at an almost jogging pace and asks for Sergeant Hank Rockwell.

'That's me,' I say, 'And you are?'

She shoves a warrant card in front of my eyes and says, 'DC Amanda Walsh, I'm your new partner.'

Totally thrown by the presence of the woman, dressed in elegant navy-blue trousers and a blue blouse, and this information, I stand rigid, waiting for more.

'Sorry but I was only advised this morning. I'm from the Penrith station and somebody thought I'd be closer to Katoomba than other detectives.'

'Pity they didn't use that logic for me,' I say, amused by this chain of events. 'Where's Andrew, my usual partner?'

'I'm sorry sir. I don't know.' Amanda stares at me as though she's awaiting an instruction.

'Never mind,' I say. 'Come with me and don't talk until I ask you to.' I lead her to the two uniforms. 'Hi, I'm DS Rockwell. I understand you met with the people who found the body.'

'That's right,' says the taller of the two men. 'Here, I've written the details down.'

I peer at the note and record the information in the notes app on my phone. Then turning to Amanda, I say, 'Want to see the body?'

'What? I 'm fine sir.'

DC Walsh doesn't want to see the blood and guts, I glean from her response and body language. But she's in Homicide now and needs to be introduced to the gory bits as well as the fun bits of detective work. Not that there are fun bits in this work.

'Just pop inside and you'll see we're dealing with a murder. You don't faint, do you?'

'No sir.' She trots off and disappears into the cabin to do as suggested. While she is coming to grips with the sight of the victim, I stand near the pool, gazing at the water and wondering how often the hotel cleans it. I wouldn't dive into that germ-infested cesspool if you paid me.

Amanda comes out a moment later, hand over mouth, as though she is protecting herself from vomiting. She doesn't speak, simply looks at me.

'Okay, follow me. You can talk whenever you want now,' I say, trying to assess what she is made of.

I knock on a door on a room on the first floor of the hotel, after having shown my warrant card to reception and asking for Ray Saunders. When nothing happens, I pound my fists on the door and shout 'Police, open up.'

The door opens a moment later, and I see a stout fair-haired man with eyes half closed and straggly hair bunched up over his head, bits pointing everywhere. Reminds me of a guy I knew with heaps of hair swept up by a gale force wind. 'Yeah?' The man asks.

'You're Mr Saunders?'

He nods.

'I'm DS Rockwell and this is DC Walsh. May we come in?'

'Do you know what time it is?' says Saunders.

I smile. 'Well aware, sir.'

He lets us in and we see a young woman still in bed. 'What's happening?' she asks.

'Don't be alarmed,' I say, 'we're here to ask about the body you chanced upon.'

'Oh yeah,' says Saunders, 'Julie suggested calling the cops.'

'Good decision,' I say. Saunders, Amanda and I stand at the foot of the bed, peering at Julie. She has brown mousey hair and sports freckles on her face. 'Can you tell us exactly how you stumbled upon the body?'

Saunders sits on the bed next to his companion. He takes her hand in his. 'Julie and I went for a walk and we noticed a cabin opposite the pool with the light on. We went to see whether the occupants were going to go for a swim which we wanted to do. I knocked but noticed the door was not closed completely. So, when I pushed the door a little more, it opened up fully. At first I didn't know whether to walk in or not. I called out but there was no response so I did walk in. That's when we saw the dead guy, didn't we hon?'

Julie looks at Saunders then at us. 'Yeah, like we went to knock again like, then we found the door was open like.'

'Why did you go out so early in the morning?' Amanda asks.

I glance at Amanda. A good question, one I was going to raise but I'm pleased she's asked it. I'm still befuddled by the senior brass's decision to have her become my partner for this assignment. Even in her uniform-like clothing, she still looks prettier than either Andrew Banks or his mousey partner or most police colleagues. That's for sure, I think, returning my eyes to the witnesses. I need to keep my mind on the job, I realise, and not be distracted by the new detective's appearance or mannerisms.

'We thought it would be fun. It was just after three and we'd been dancing so we didn't think it was too late. Right hon?' Saunders lets go of Julie's hand.

'Yeah, like it would be less crowded at that time we figured,' agrees Julie.

'Why did you need to have somebody join you?' I look at Saunders as Julie seems likely to agree with her male companion.

'Just thought it would be a hoot. We were going to skinny dip, so I wanted to make sure that was okay with the other couple should they appear. At the time, we didn't know the cabin was only the guy's digs.'

'Did you see anyone else around at that time?' I ask, amused by the man's messy hair as he tries to get it to straighten.

'No, no one.'

'Thank you for your time, Mr and Mrs Saunders,' I say.

'We're not married,' says Julie, 'I'm Julie Thornton.'

'Okay, have fun,' I reply. I wanted to know as much as I could about the couple in case we needed to come back with further questions. My motto is to never assume anything.

As I walk back down the steps, I invite Amanda to join me for a coffee. Being a popular resort hotel, I expect them to serve decent coffee. We find the lounge in the Hydro Majestic and order. I also want a chance to talk to Amanda and suss out what she is like.

'Did you believe the couple?' I ask.

'I think they were honest. The only thing I couldn't figure was the delay in getting the call. They were outside the pool at roughly three to three-thirty, found the body a little later and I got a call at six.'

'Probably took time for the system to alert the right areas. The Katoomba cops did arrive earlier than anyone.' So I was told when I arrived.

Coffees arrive. I'm saved. Without my morning hit, I can get testy.

'Would you like something else?' asks the waitress.

'Perhaps in a moment,' I say. I watch as the mature brunette wanders off. Breakfast would be nice but I'm not ready for it yet. Turning back to Amanda, I say, 'We'll hope to get something from

Forensics, fingerprints on the knife would be great but I'm not expecting such luck. In the meantime, we'll have to find out all we can about the victim. Are you okay with that?'

'You're the boss,' says Amanda.

Music to my ears. I don't cope well with argumentative types. We have coffee and Amanda orders breakfast. As I consume my coffee, I suggest a plan.

At the check-in desk, I ask whether Brent Morton, the name on the victim's driver's licence, checked in by himself or with somebody else.

The receptionist says she can't disclose that information because of privacy concerns which the hotel takes very seriously.

I present my warrant card as this receptionist is different from the one I quizzed previously, the one who gave me the number of the Saunders room. 'You should know this is a murder investigation and the bloke I'm referring to isn't going to worry about privacy. He's dead. He's not going to worry about anything else, for that matter.'

'Oh, right. Let me see.' She checks something. She's tall, slim and dumb, as far as I can tell. I notice Amanda looking strangely at me. Probably doesn't approve of my operational style which could be more polite, less confrontational, but I don't care. I've never been into being popular. Even at school, I was sarcastic and at times, abrasive. This meant I had less friends than the popular girls and boys, but my friends lasted. To this day, I still have two good solid friends from high school, ones whom I can count on through thick and thin.

But I don't have female friends or wives or partners. Always pissed them off. So, I wonder how long it will be before Amanda will ask to be transferred away from me. A day, a week; I'll see. Yet I like women but often I put my foot in it when I'm dating a woman or during the relationship. At least Andrew, my usual detective partner, knows I'm a son of a bitch, and he accepts me for who I am.

The receptionist, who looks too young to be working at anything except being an assistant to an assistant, looks up. 'He came with a lady,' she says.

'Name and room number,' I say wondering how slow can she be.

She looks down again, then back to me. 'Her name is Candice Berry and she has a cabin next to his, I mean next to the man who died. He agreed to pay both bills, so I don't know why they booked separate rooms.'

'Thanks, Sarah,' I say looking at her nametag. 'Much appreciated.' At least Mr Morton won't need to pay for either room now. Being dead clears all debts and worries.

I update Amanda with the information as she was waiting a few metres back from the desk. We walk outside and wander to the door next to Brent Morton's. I see the Forensic team is packing up. I walk up to Ho. 'Sam, when can you give me your findings?'

'I'll push it through mate. You owe me a few beers.'

'No problem. Thanks. See you,' I say patting him on the back.

Brent Morton's cabin has been sealed with police tape to preserve it as a crime scene. The uniforms ask whether they're still needed. I tell them they can go once the body has been removed and sent to the mortuary.

I return to Amanda's side. She is standing outside Ms Berry's room, looking at something on her phone. I wink at her then knock on the door.

TWO

Candice

WHEN A WOMAN IN HER thirties opens the door, she looks sleepy. Although she only wears a T-shirt, I can see she has more curves than the winding section of Military Road in Mosman. She yawns, 'What's up?'

I show her my warrant card, 'Ms Berry?' The T-shirt is white with the words "Girl Power" in bold in front. The garment just covers her buttocks.

'Yes.'

'I'm DS Hank Rockwell and this is DC Amanda Walsh. May we come in?'

'Okay,' says Candice and walks ahead while we follow. She sits on the bed, crosses one shapely leg over the other, and points to two chairs which she indicates we could use. Pulling one chair closer to the bed, I sit directly in front of Candice and Amanda sits to my right. I look into Candice's eyes, trying hard not to let my gaze drift down to her enormous bust. The T-shirt is stretched to breaking point.

'Ms Berry...'

'Call me Candy,' she says.

'Okay,' I say, 'I have some bad news. Your boyfriend Brent is dead.'

'What? You're kidding. I only saw him a few hours ago,' she shrieks. 'What happened?'

I know I'm no diplomat and won't be called upon to represent the country in one of our overseas embassies, but I find her reaction tough to handle. Although I've spoken to other bereaved family members, I prefer to let others manage it. I'm about to tell her Brent's been murdered but decide to let Amanda deal with it, woman to woman. I glance at her and nod imperceptibly, hoping she gets my meaning.

Amanda rises to the occasion. 'A guest found Mr Morton lying on the floor of his cabin. He'd been stabbed in the neck.'

"He was murdered?"

A bright girl, I think, realising knives generally don't implant themselves without some help.

Candice gets up, grabs a tissue from the counter and blows her nose. Then she tosses it into a waste basket. Before she returns to the bed, Candice pulls another tissue from the box and dabs her eyes dry. 'Oh my God. I can't believe it.'

'What were your movements last night?' Diplomacy over, I can re-enter the fray.

'We were all in Brent's room, talking, having a few drinks and skinny dipping in the pool. He was alive when we left, I swear.'

'Who else was in the room?' I ask. I see Amanda take out a notepad from her side pocket and a pen from the pocket at the top of her blouse. She might work out, I think. As a detective.

'Grant and Fiona and Mitch and Sally,' Candice says, sobbing again. 'Who would hurt Brent?'

'Six of you?' I confirm, ignoring her question. Obviously, somebody had it in for Brent.

'Yes, we're best friends, all of us. Have you arrested anyone?'

I love her faith in the police. 'Not yet,' I say.

'If he's your boyfriend, why separate rooms?' Amanda asks.

'He's not my boyfriend, although we have slept together. We're just friends, ever since university.'

'Tell us exactly what happened last night,' I say, not keen to dig into their romantic entanglements, just yet. I stand to stretch my legs and ask whether I could have a bottle of cold water.

'Sure. Take one from the minibar,' says Candice who has finished crying.

I open the minibar and note it is stocked with alcohol, soft drinks and water bottles. I take a bottle of still water and check whether any drugs are stored in the fridge. I sit down. 'Did you do coke or ecstasy last night?'

'Are you going to bust us for that?'

'No Candy,' I say, 'Merely establishing the scene. Okay, last night. Start from the beginning.'

Amanda and I listen while Candice tells her story. The six friends arrived in three vehicles. Mitch and Sally arrived first, and they shared a room. They're more than best friends, it appears, having dated for a couple of years. Then Brent and Candice arrived in Brent's Toyota Hilux and the couple checked into separate poolside rooms. Finally, the perennially late Grant arrives with Fiona in a Porsche. The group meet for drinks, having kept in touch by phone. Then they adjourn to the dining room and eat dinner. The hotel had a buffet on Friday night which the friends knew about beforehand and they'd planned to indulge themselves after a stressful week at work. The friends then listened to a band and throughout the evening danced with various partners. After midnight they went to Brent's room, drank and participated in sharing weed, then went swimming. Candice left Brent's room last. It was ten minutes to two o'clock. She remembers this because she slipped, caught herself on the door to her place and saw the time on her watch.

'That's it?' I look at Candice, wondering if she's telling the complete story. 'No arguments or hassles?'

'Oh yes, I forgot. In the dance hall, Brent had a barney with another guest, but I don't know what it was about.'

'Which guest?'

'I don't know,' says Candice, 'some drunken bloke as I recall. A big guy.'

'You can't remember what he looked like?' Amanda queries.

'Sorry. I wasn't paying much attention as I was chatting with Fiona. Noticed some pushing and raised voices, that's all.'

'Could any of your friends have returned to visit Brent?'

Candice glares at me. 'What? Do you think one of our friends killed Brent? That's not possible.'

'Calm down Candy, we know very little at this stage and we're obliged to cover all possibilities. I'm not accusing anyone,' I say. Candice might have a very fuckable body but her hysterical personality would turn me off. I could just imagine being near a climax with her and suddenly she remembers she forgot to water the plants and goes apeshit.

'Are you okay Candy? Would you like me to get a doctor to prescribe a sedative?' asks the caring Amanda.

'I'm fine. I have some Valium. Thanks anyway,' says Candice.

Accepting that we need to take a break and return to Candice later when she's recovered from shock, I say, 'We'll leave you alone now. Thanks for your assistance. We'll pop back a little later, give you time to rest. Are your friends next door?'

'Yes. Grant and Fiona are to my right and to their right are Mitch and Sally.' Candice puts her arms around herself as though she's cold.

Amanda and I step outside. For the first time today, I can observe the environment. The sky is cloudless, and the temperature feels warm. The day is threatening to be a hot one as time progresses throughout the day. I suggest to Amanda that we take a walk before tackling our next couple. Now that I'm fully awake, I can appreciate the beauty of the hotel. The external structure is impressive. Huge. White. Looks almost like some kind of palace.

As we wander past the reception entrance, I turn to Amanda. 'Thoughts?'

'Hopefully, one of the friends can tell us more about the scuffle Brent had on the dance floor,' says Amanda as she watches her step moving along the uneven pavement taking us around to the back of the hotel which gives us a view of bushland, the wonderful sight featuring a valley full of trees and other forms of greenery. I was never into botany.

'I wouldn't mind another coffee,' I say, pleased Amanda has been paying attention. 'But it can wait. Let's tackle Grant and Fiona first.'

THREE

Fiona

WHEN I KNOCK ON THE solid door to the cabin next door to Candice's accommodation, a woman appears almost immediately. She is tall, slim and blonde. The short cut-off jeans reveal beautiful long legs, flawless and smooth. She also has a white low-cut blouse, but she has no boobs to speak of. The very opposite of Candice's upper body.

'Hello, what can I do for you?' she asks in a cultured accent. An accent which is Australian but modified, I recognise, by having spent time in England.

'Fiona?' I ask, looking into blue eyes.

'Yes.'

I show her my warrant card and introduce Amanda and ask whether we could speak with her and her companion.

'I'm afraid Grant isn't here. He's gone for breakfast. I didn't join him as I don't eat breakfast,' Fiona says.

'The secret to keeping slim?' Amanda asks.

Fiona smiles. 'Not really. I just don't like breakfast.'

Fiona invites us in and we sit in a circle with Fiona on the bed, legs crossed elegantly. Her cabin is neat and clean looking. Candice's was messy in comparison with clothes and bags visible on the floor and benches. Brent's cabin was even messier but then he was dead and not interested in being tidy.

We ask Fiona about the previous day after informing her that Brent was found murdered. She showed surprise and shock but understood we were here to do our job. I mention we would record the conversation as this would be her official statement. When we informed Candice of this, she had no issues with the process.

Looking at me but also at Amanda occasionally, she tells her story.

> *Grant and I have been friends since university. He studied commerce and I did an Arts degree which I discovered was useless in the job market, but I managed to obtain some useful work for companies as a personal assistant. It might seem like a lowly job given my qualifications, but I ended up enjoying it. He helped me in with getting a job in my two-year stint in London and now that I'm back, just six months ago, I have a very good position with a legal practice. Anyway, I reconnected with Grant on my return. While I was travelling overseas, he'd kept in touch with me as did Mitch, Brent, Candy and Sally.*
>
> *Yesterday Grant collected me from my flat in Waverton in his Porsche 911, a beautiful silver car, and we drove up to the Hydro. It's a lovely spot, isn't it? So, we checked in together in this poolside cabin. We're a couple now, have been for a couple of months, and it was a great opportunity to get away and relax. All of us agreed to take the Friday and Monday off work so we could enjoy an extended weekend here.*
>
> *We had dinner in the dining room with the spectacular view out over the valley. Grant just loves the various public rooms and corridors at the hotel. He's a very sensitive person and has a fine sense of style. He can look at art for hours. Loves paintings by the impressionists. Anyway, we dined then went to listen to the band. Brent and Candy danced while Mitch and Sally sat around, drinking beers and wine. Grant and I had the occasional dance but also enjoyed chatting and having some laughs.*
>
> *Later we adjourned to Brent's room. That's where the fun began. We smoked some grass and went swimming, naked. We were the only ones using the pool, so we could indulge ourselves and remain nude. It felt wicked but lovely.*

'What time did you go back to your room?' I ask when I figure Fiona has finished.

'God…I don't know…around one-twenty or thirty I think.'

'How did Brent appear?'

'Out of it. He seemed stoned, but I can't be sure, he often looks like a zombie even when he's not had any drugs or alcohol,' says Fiona.

Fiona is so distracting particularly when she crosses and uncrosses those lovely long legs, so silky, so slim that I have to take a deep breath. So, I say, to keep my mind focused on the case. 'You don't like him, do you?'

'That's perceptive. How did you know. He was an arrogant bastard.'

That hit a nerve. But I can't see her as a killer unless she had been involved with him. 'Did you two ever fuck?'

Fiona looks aghast. Amanda utters something signifying shock at the words I chose. Surely, I could have said 'sleep with him' I can see her thinking to herself. But I'm the boss, as she's confirmed.

'Well?' I insist.

'Yes,' says Fiona. 'He forced himself on me at a party years ago. I was so weak, I gave in to him. It was terrible. I hated it.'

'You only slept with him once then?' Amanda asks, using language which is probably more acceptable to Fiona.

'No, a few times but I broke it off. He was an unpleasant man. I shudder when I think of it.'

'I'm puzzled,' I say, 'If he, as you said, forced himself onto you, why didn't you report the incident to the police?'

'I don't know…I thought about it but before I had the confidence, he apologised. And he bought a gift for me. But he was horrible and when I came to my senses, it was too late.' Fiona rubbed her nose and returned eye contact.

'Okay, thanks Ms. Harrison,' I say, 'We'll leave you alone now. We'd like to talk to Grant too. Will you inform him please? DC

Walsh and I will be having a coffee, should he return in the next little while?'

'Of course.' Fiona stands, and I shake her hand. I have an impulse to brush my lips over her slender fingers, but I've caused her enough of a shock for the moment. Besides, I'm not French or Italian.

FOUR

Grant

As I'm finishing my second mug of Cappuccino for the day, a slender man approaches our table. He is just short of six foot, I guess, a fraction shorter than me, with short dark hair and he's clean shaven, even on a weekend. He's wearing dark blue Pierre Cardin chino shorts and a short-sleeved collared white shirt. He looks fashionable and elegant and he seems a perfect fit for the slim and delectable Fiona. Amanda looks at him and I sense a kind of attraction. She has certainly not shown the same level of interest towards me. Is there no chemistry between Amanda and me, I wonder, as I survey our guest? Perhaps I'm too rugged for her with my two-day bristle and world-worn almost forty-year-old face. During our coffees, Amanda and I had been discussing our interview with Fiona and both of us have come to the conclusion Fiona had a motive to want Brent dead but was unlikely to kill him for an affair now a decade old.

'Hi, I'm Grant Michaels. I understand from Fiona you'd like to talk with me.'

'Hello Grant,' I say standing and shaking his hand, 'Thank you for coming to us to provide your statement. Please take a seat. I'm DS Hank Rockwell and this is DC Amanda Walsh.'

'Nice to meet you,' Grant says, looking at Amanda and smiling. 'Now, how can I help?'

'We'd appreciate your account of what happened last night,' I tell him, sitting down and switching my phone onto the record function then placing it on the centre of the table. 'I hope you don't mind us recording this interview. Saves note taking for which my associate is not prepared.' Amanda is prepared but I want to record his words exactly.

'That's fine, I have nothing to hide,' he says.

'Great,' I look at Amanda to see that she's on board with my approach. She doesn't react, keeping a straight face.

Grant makes himself comfortable on a chair, his back to the spectacular view of nature outside, perhaps to prevent distraction. He appears to me to be a serious person. He tells his story, his eyes moving between myself and Amanda.

> *Fiona and I arrived up here around five o'clock yesterday. We checked in, then I took the luggage out of the vehicle and set up the room for the three full days we would be here. I called Mitch to arrange a get together for drinks before dinner. The six of us, all of us good friends, met and had drinks at the Salon du, then dined in the Wintergarden Restaurant. It was a fine dining experience and I found that Fiona really enjoyed it. Fiona and I left the group to take an evening stroll which aids digestion and also to spend some time alone. We re-joined the group in the Boiler Room where we listened to the live band and danced. Brent was dancing with Sally when an argument occurred between him and another guest. I don't know what it was about, but it didn't spill over into a physical fight. Later we went to Brent's room and had a swim. Fiona and I left a little after one. I'd had a big week at work, a very tense and stressful time, putting a deal together, so I wanted to call it a night. That's all I can recall.*

I watched Grant closely as he told the story which seemed coherent. But I sensed it was prepared in advance. I don't know why I felt this; it showed attention to most of the things we might ask. Almost as though it covered everything we might want to know. So,

I ask a question he may not have thought about. 'Who's your best friend?'

'Fiona, of course.'

'She's your girlfriend so that doesn't count. She told us you were all good friends.'

'That's right,' Grant says as he shifts in his chair. As a waitress serves a guest and stands close to our table, he signals to her and asks for a herbal tea. I order another coffee. Amanda shakes her head when the waitress, a woman in her thirties with a fair-haired bun atop her head, enquires whether she'd like something.

'Mr Michaels, getting back to my question, which one of the group is your best friend, other than Fiona?'

'Hard to say. I like them all.'

'What about your best mate?'

'The six of us were all friends at uni, but since then I have moved on and I have a best mate at the investment bank I work for. His name is Josh. I don't know why you need to know this.'

'No reason,' I say, 'I thought it may not have been Brent.'

'I don't get it.' Michaels seems a little uncomfortable, twisting in his chair a fraction.

The beverages we ordered a moment ago are served to us by the same efficient big-bottomed waitress, several tattoos evident on her arms.

'You don't seem too distressed by his death,' I say, watching his expression. I've found in the past that questions out of left field can sometimes elicit telling responses.

'I'm devastated. Fiona is too and I'm sure the others are just as much. I just don't show emotion as much as others. But inside, I'm choked. The whole business is terrible. He was a good friend.'

'Thanks, Grant. I'll let you go to try to enjoy the rest of your time here.'

'With what's happened to Brent, I don't think Fiona, or I want to continue staying here,' says Grant, smoothing the front of his shirt. He pushes his tea aside, only half finished.

'I get it, but we'd like you to hang around until our enquiries are over,' I say. Then just as Grant stands, I ask, 'Oh, Grant, can you describe the guy Brent argued with on the dancefloor?'

'Sure. He wore a checked shirt. Blue, I think. Big guy with blonde hair.'

'Thanks for your help.'

Grant walks off and I can see his stride is more hurried than when he came into the restaurant. I drink the rest of my coffee.

'What did you make of that interview? You didn't ask any questions, I noted.'

Amanda grins. 'I couldn't have added anything. All the matters we needed seemed to be covered. Why did you give Grant such a hard time?'

'No reason really. I felt he was a little too smooth, so I wanted to ruffle his feathers a little.'

'Like you do with me,' says Amanda.

'Ha, is that what you think? Are you ready to check out the last couple?'

'What about the guy on the dancefloor?'

'Don't worry, we'll work on that too,' I shove my empty cup towards the centre of the table. I pick up my iPhone, switch off the recording function and pocket it.

'Have you had enough coffee?' Amanda asks.

"Don't know,' I say, pushing my hand through my hair. Something is bothering me. I peer at the vista outside and my thoughts crystalize. 'Fiona never mentioned the altercation on the dance floor, did you notice?'

'You're right. Maybe it didn't impact on her.'

'Or she neglected to tell us,' I point out.

FIVE

Mitch

As AMANDA AND I WALK back towards the pool, I sight Ms Hysterical, with the cup size in lower levels of the alphabet, talking to a bearded man who is smoking a cigarette. She sees us and waves. We walk over.

'Hi there,' Candice says, 'This is Mitch who is absolutely devastated about Brent's death. When I told him, clear shock registered on his face.'

'Hello Mitch,' I say extending my hand, but he doesn't bother shaking it, 'I'm…'

'I know,' he says, 'cops.'

'That's right. We'd like to talk to you.' I'm not amused by his attitude. A cop hater.

Mitch draws on his cigarette, exhaling a huge amount of smoke. I wonder whether he's aware of the risks. I doubt he'd take much notice anyway. His attitude suggests he's stubborn and that he wouldn't do anything except what he wants to do. 'It's not convenient at the moment, as you can see. I'm chatting to my mate's girlfriend.'

'Okay, would you rather us take you to the station?' I ask, considering whether it would be best to transport him to the Katoomba or Penrith police branches.

'You can't do that. I haven't done anything,' says the broad shouldered short man. He tosses the cigarette butt on the ground and steps on it.

'I can arrest you for obstructing a murder investigation. So what is it Mr…?

'Norris,' he says.

'Well, what's it to be?' I'm getting annoyed and ready to arrest him and drag him away. Although he's powerful looking, I know how to subdue most people physically as I'm a black belt in karate and I've had some UFC (Ultimate Fighting Championship) fights, all successful. I'm a mean son-of-a-bitch when I want to be.

'Alright, let's talk here,' says Mitch.

'Not here, let's go somewhere private,' I say, 'do you mind Candy?'

'Fine with me,' says Candice who is dressed in black leggings and a sleeveless T-shirt which is stretched to breaking point over her torso. I'm no judge but I'd imagine she'd be an F or G cup bra size. I hope Amanda doesn't see me observing Candice's top. I'm embarrassed by my fascination with her breasts but I can't help it. I'm only human. I now appreciate what alcoholics must suffer with their drink addiction. She walks off saying as she goes, 'See ya.'

Mitch Norris, Amanda and I adjourn to Mitch's cabin. On the way, I see that the police tape is still in place around Brent's room and I wonder whether the body has been removed. I suspect it has as there is no trace of the uniformed cops.

Inside a fairly untidy unit, clothes strewn about, I wonder how hygienic the place is.

'Sally's out,' says Mitch, 'she's gone to see her mother who lives in Leura. Will you want to talk to her?'

'Yes, but let's chat with you first,' I say as we settle in chairs with Mitch sitting on an unmade bed, covers dumped on the floor.

After some preliminaries advising him to ignore what Candice said, I ask him to tell us exactly where he was between two and three in the morning and how the night panned out for him and Sally. His story is told slowly, during breaks, it seems, as he is getting fluid intake from one bottle of beer after another. Amanda uses her phone to record the conversation.

Brent and I were best mates. We played footy at uni for a year before Brent dropped out and went to work for a plumbing company. We still hung out and had drinks every week on Friday night. So it pisses me off that somebody killed him and if I get my hands on the bastard, he'll be sorry. Anyhow, Sally and I, we're married you know, drove up here to Medlow Bath to join our best friends for a super weekend, an extended one at that. Bloody spoilt now, isn't it? Well Sally and I had pre-dinner drinks after checking in. All the group was there with Grant and Fiona arriving last. Then we had dinner together. Sally's vegan but the restaurant catered for that. Great place. Music and dancing after that. Brent likes to dance, I mean liked to dance, and he got all the girls up at some stage. Fiona had a dance before sitting down again but Sally had an extended go. I didn't mind, gave me a chance to have a few more beers without being nagged. Then we made our way to Brent's cabin individually. I was last as I wanted to finish my drink. As I got there some of the gang had already stripped and were in the pool. Brent and I had a smoke then joined in. All I remember after that was being in bed. Sally was beside me in the morning, so I figured all was well.

Listening to Mitch's story, I gained the distinct impression he was an alcoholic, a functioning alcoholic perhaps, but one nonetheless. 'Thanks for that. So, you don't know where you were between two and three?'

'Not exactly, no,' says Mitch who gets up and grabs another beer from the fridge. 'Would either of you like a drink?'

'No thanks,' says Amanda, 'we're on duty.'

'That's what I thought,' says Mitch going back to the edge of the bed and sitting down.

'How long have you and Sally been married?' I query.

'A long time. Fuck I can't remember. She'd know.'

'Did you see Brent argue with someone on the dance floor?' asks Amanda.

'Oh yeah. I saw a bloke push him but Brent shoved him and then they seemed to resort to just arguing. I was ready to go to Brent's aid if it got physical and kick the guy's arse but nothing more eventuated.'

Amanda carries on, keen to find this dance floor bully. 'Could you describe him?'

'Big but that's all I recall.' Mitch takes another gulp of beer. The bottle is now only a quarter full.

I stand up, not bothering to shake the man's hand. Soon he won't be able to stand properly, I figure. "Thanks Mr Norris, please make sure you stay at the hotel until we advise it's okay to go. Let Sally know we want to talk to her too. Here's my card. By the way, what do you do for a living?'

'I'm in IT. I work freelance.'

I open the door and let Amanda precede me.

Outside, I walk ahead of her until we get a fair distance from the cabin. 'What do you make of him?'

'A sad case. I doubt he'd remember if he stabbed his so-called buddy.'

'True, but he wouldn't have the presence of mind to wipe the blade clean of fingerprints.'

'Were no fingerprints found?'

'Don't know but I bet whoever did it wiped the prints. I'll get a report Monday morning,' I say. It would be too much to expect the case would be so easily solved. My cynical nature prevents me from accepting crime or life, for that matter, is easily negotiated.

'What now?' asks Amanda.

'Lunch. What do you say?'

'Okay. Plenty of choice here.'

'What do you like to be called, Mandy or Amanda or Detective Constable or something else?'

'I'm okay with Amanda,' says Amanda who sports an amused expression. 'Are you becoming considerate all of a sudden?'

'Touché.' I'm beginning to warm to her.

We pop into Darley's Restaurant, one of the many eating spots in the hotel, and take a seat near the window which has a great view of mountains. In the distance they appear blue which is probably why this region is called the Blue Mountains. Very clever.

We sit opposite each other and I look at Amanda more closely. She has piercing hazel eyes, olive skin and short jet-black hair. She looks a bit like Demi Lovato. Beautiful. Why hadn't I noticed before? I had a lot on my mind, I tell myself. But with Candice and Fiona and Amanda, I'm going nuts. I can only hope Sally is ugly. I shake my head so that my stare disappears and I say, to cover myself, 'Sorry, I was deep in thought. Hope you didn't think I was looking right through you.'

'Do you suspect anyone yet?'

'I suspect everybody. In my experience, it's good to work on a list of key suspects but more often than not, the guilty person turns out to be someone you never envisaged originally.'

'I see. I've not worked on a murder investigation before, but I can't see an obvious killer, other than the dance hall bully.'

'Okay. We'll find him and speak with him. I'm also not excluding Candice, the girlfriend. She seems to have quite an emotional streak, so I wouldn't put it past her to have stabbed her boyfriend in a fit of rage.'

'About what?'

'I have no idea.'

SIX

Sally

SALLY IS NOTHING LIKE I imagined. For a guy like Mitch, I thought his wife would be chunky or substantial or at least odd looking. But no. When Sally finally meets with us in a café in Leura, she breaks all the rules of my imagination. She is tiny. Barely five foot tall and slim. In fact, her most prominent feature is her frizzy hair, fair with a purple streak through it.

The reason we're meeting in Leura is because Sally wanted to stay with her mother that night. We only found out because Amanda who has been surprisingly efficient had obtained Mitch's mobile phone then enquired about Sally's number. Collecting mobiles is something we need to do with all the friends as they are all suspects in Brent's murder.

We are all seated around a round wooden table in Sally's favourite café and I order another coffee, my umpteenth for the day. Amanda, sensible Amanda, orders spring water and Sally asks for tea. I wonder whether she and Grant get together for afternoon tea sometimes, but I don't utter these words.

'Thanks for meeting with us Mrs Norris,' I say after going through the ritual of formerly introducing ourselves and showing our warrant cards.

'That's okay. Call me Sally please. I get Mrs at school all day long,' says Sally.

'You're a teacher?' says Amanda.

'Primary school, yes. How can I be of assistance?' Sally brushes hair off her forehead.

I explain about Brent being found murdered. I don't provide details of the murder, leaving the details open to see if somebody inadvertently mentions facts.

'Oh my God, that's terrible. He was only three doors down from us. Who did it?'

'That's what we're working on,' I say. 'Would you tell us about your movements yesterday and this morning?'

Sally waits for our drinks delivery which the waitress is currently placing in front of us. Then, sipping tea from time to time, she tells her story. Amanda records the session after gaining permission from Sally.

> *Mitch and I left our house in Eastwood early, can't remember the time but we drove slowly and stopped off to have breakfast. We unpacked when we got to the Hydro then sat down and relaxed for a moment. We joined the others for drinks then dinner. Everyone was in a good mood, talking about their week, the fact we don't see each other enough and making jokes. It was fun. Mitch and I rarely go out these days. Together, I mean. He still goes to the pub and meets Brent…I mean, met Brent. Oh, how tragic. I don't know how Mitch is going to cope with his best mate gone.*
>
> *After dinner, the girls visited the ladies and we caught up with the lads at the Boiler House where we drank and danced. Oh yes, I danced with Brent when he accidentally stepped on the toes of this bloke's woman. Well, you should have seen the reaction. Brent apologised but the man, a big brute of a fellow, pushed Brent and told him to watch himself. Brent stood up for himself and soon the two squared off as if to fight. But it never came to that. Harsh words were exchanged and this was enough, it seemed. I was a bit shaken up and I asked Brent to sit down again. But he wasn't going to be intimidated by anyone and we carried on dancing. We left the dance floor soon after the big guy and his wife*

departed. After some more drinks the gang went to Brent's room, not as a group but in dribs and drabs. We had more drinks in the cabin and then some of us went skinny dipping. I didn't drink that much but the boys certainly did. Mitch and I headed back to our place at one twenty. Mitch fell into bed with his clothes on and didn't stir until the morning, around seven o'clock when I went to the bathroom.

'An eventful evening,' Amanda says.

'Yes, it was.'

'So, Brent was alive when you left at 1:20?' I ask.

'Definitely. I remember him pecking me on the cheek when I said goodnight.'

'Have you ever slept with him?' I ask.

'At university but that was a long time ago. We're all thirty-five now. Water under the bridge,' says Sally pouring more tea into her cup.

'Was Mitch jealous?'

'No. He never knew. I took up with Mitch afterwards. In fact, I met Mitch through Brent. He wouldn't have killed him for that. It's crazy and besides Mitch was too far gone this morning to do anything, let alone last night when he wouldn't be able to stand up.'

'Can you describe the man who argued with Brent, you know, on the dance floor?' asks Amanda.

'Sandy hair, big snoz, wore black jeans and a blue checked shirt,' says Sally. 'And he was broad and taller than Brent. So maybe six foot four.'

'What about the lady?' Amanda presses.

'Funny, she was short like me with a black backless dress and she was a brunette.'

'Thanks,' says Amanda, 'are you going back to the Hydro tomorrow?'

'Yes. Mum's not been well, so I'll spend some time with her today. And Mitch can't go far. I've got the car.'

Amanda explains that we need her mobile.

'What am I going to use?'

'Perhaps you can buy a burner,' I suggest.

Sally is clearly unhappy but she passes her phone to Amanda who now has all the phones except Brent's which nobody could find.

As we've now all finished our drinks, I stand, shake Sally's hand, and thank her for the statement and the time she spent with us. I escort Amanda back to my two-year old Holden Commodore. I drive back to the Hydro Majestic, not saying much until we're about half-way there. Amanda too is deep in thought. I change the radio to a CD track. Playing is a Moody Blues album.

'What do you like, music wise?' I ask.

'George Ezra, Rita Ora. Modern stuff,' says Amanda.

'How old are you?'

'Old enough to know not to reveal my age,' says Amanda with a cheeky grin.

'You realise I could easily find out,' I say.

'Naturally. You're a detective, aren't you?'

'Don't worry, I won't. You probably like hip hop too.'

'Some.'

I continue my silence for another ten minutes.

'Next we'll speak with your favourite suspect, the dance hall bully,' I say peeking at Amanda.

'Just thought we should follow up,' says Amanda.

'Absolutely right,' I say, not telling her she's doing exactly what should be done. I may have to praise her later, if our enquiries lead to something positive. In the meantime, I'll keep an open mind.

'Are we going to ask reception whether they know of a tall guy staying at the hotel?'

'Now you're being silly. I'm going to have you stand at the exit until you spot him,' I say, feeling mischievous.

'Right,' says Amanda, her sarcastic tone not lost on me.

'The sky's darkening. Might get some rain,' I say.

'When do you think we should head back?'

'I don't know. Let's continue our interviews before we come up with a plan.'

Once I've parked the car, we wander to reception and I see there's another person manning the desk. It's a man who looks mature, around fifty.

'Hello,' I say, 'I'm DS Rockwell. Last night there was a bit of a scuffle in the Boiler House, the music venue, I believe.'

'Yes sir there was,' says Malcolm, his name displayed on his nametag.

'Do you know who the guests were?'

'Yes sir. Brent Morton and Herb Petrov.'

'How did you establish this?'

'One of our security staff went over to them afterwards to ask what the problem was and asked for their names. We have a safety-first policy and we wouldn't be doing our job if we allowed brawling,' says Malcolm as he brushes away a spot on his jacket.

'Thank you. May I have Mr Petrov's room number?'

SEVEN

Dance Hall Bully

As we climb the stairs to Herb Petrov's room, I question why a man would commit murder after a slight altercation. I've known of pub fights which ended in murder and domestics where drink or emotion have played a part, but I cannot recall a situation where somebody planned and committed a murder after something as trivial as a bump against a stranger. If the parties had decided to fight or if somebody humiliated the other, then there is a possibility further action might have been taken.

Amanda knocks on the door to room 111. After repeated attempts and no response, she accepts that nobody is in.

'Should we leave a card with a message?' Amanda asks.

'No. We don't want to alert him,' I say. 'He hasn't checked out. I checked. We'll try later. In the meantime, I might get you to have all six of the friends put through the system for priors.'

'Yes sir,' says Amanda.

'No need to call me sir. My name's Rockwell or Hank, whichever you prefer.'

'I'll go to the car and organise it. Anything else?'

'Try Herb Petrov as well. He could be in the system if he's got a short fuse.'

'Okay.'

'Before you go, I thought we might stay here overnight. Driving back and forth doesn't make sense. Any problem with that?'

'No s…Hank.'

'I'll book us rooms while you talk to your colleagues.'

Amanda leaves the hotel while I return to reception.

Just as I've finished booking two rooms, a short woman followed by a tall man enters the hotel. They walk towards the stairs. I wait for Amanda and then we go back to room 111. This time the door opens to reveal a slim woman with blood red lipstick. Is she a vampire who enjoys blood for afternoon tea, I wonder.

'We'd like to talk with Mr Petrov,' I say.

'What you want with Herbie?'

I show her my warrant card. 'Just a routine few questions.'

'Come in.'

I follow the petite woman inside where we find Petrov lying on the bed. Legs crossed. 'Sofia, who are these people?'

'Police.'

'Police?'

'Ya,' Sofia says.

Petrov slides off the bed and stands, looking at me. Herb Petrov in solid tradie work boots stands at around six foot five, a couple of inches taller than me. And as he is also broad shouldered with a barrel chest, he looks imposing and not somebody to take lightly in a street brawl. We glare at each other for a few minutes and I wonder what he is thinking as he hasn't said a word to me.

'Mr Petrov,' I say to break the impasse, 'would you take a seat please. We have a couple of questions for you.'

Then without warning, Petrov slips a knife from a back pocket and comes at me. Swaying out of the way of the first strike, I slam his wrist with a karate chop, forcing the knife to drop. Then as he tries to punch me, I step back and kick him in the right shin, charge forward and headbutt him. He drops. I hear a thump and, turning, I notice Sofia has hit the floor.

Amanda stands over her then kicks a knife away. 'She was going to stab you in the back.'

'Thanks Amanda. Excellent work. Glad to have you covering my back. Let's take both of these unpleasant characters into custody. You handcuff the woman and I'll cuff this nut. Then we'll get them taken to Katoomba. I'll question them later when they've calmed down.'

'Want me to call the station?'

'Thanks. I'm tying his ankles up as well. You wait here with your pistol trained on them. I'll take care of something downstairs.'

I meet Amanda later, after the two Russians have been bundled into a paddy wagon. I inform her that I'd booked a couple of rooms for the night. 'We need to look at all the suspects' time lines tomorrow to see whether anyone of the friends was less than forthright.'

'Why do you think the Petrovs tried to kill us?'

'I don't know but I called Forensics to go through their room. See what they're hiding or if we can match their fingerprints with any in Brent's cabin. The team will be here tomorrow.'

'Perhaps they murdered Brent. They reacted wildly today,' says Amanda.

'Sure did. I wouldn't rule anything out at this point.'

'Who's going to pay for the room?'

'It'll be on my budget,' I say, handing her a key card. We're both on the first floor. Want something to eat?'

'Not now. I'll grab room service later,' says Amanda. 'See you tomorrow.'

'Sure,' I say, looking at messages on my phone.

EIGHT

Before heading to my room, I talk to reception about the vehicle that the Petrov couple had registered. Then I walk outside and examine all vehicles in the hotel's parking areas. Wandering about, I see the sky has darkened considerably and suspect we're in for a storm. Just as well Amanda and I are staying here and not driving home then returning tomorrow morning. Finally I find an old Mazda with the number plates I've been searching for. I'll make sure Forensics check this out as well. I've ensured their room 111 is also sealed off as a crime scene so that it cannot be tampered with.

A few raindrops strike my head. I hurry inside and await the magic rush of pelting rain and thunder. Although my friend's dog is frightened by loud thunder claps, I love to sit and stare out at furious weather. The sheer power of nature is liberating showing mere mortals that we can't control everything. Once inside my room, the full force of the storm has descended and I stand by the window, witnessing the scene outside. If only I had a woman to snuggle up to, the world, for me, would be perfect.

Twenty minutes later, I'm lying on the bed, contemplating dinner. I review the menu and order a hamburger. I take a beer from the fridge and wait. I switch on the television and channel surf. There's nothing of interest so I turn the screen off. I have a novel in my vehicle but decide not to bother. It's still raining. Room service arrives. I eat my burger without chips. I want to remain fit and not put on unnecessary weight from poor eating habits. It's bad enough that I enjoy and drink too much alcohol.

I'm bored and about to wander down to a bar when there's a knock on the door. I check the peephole before resorting to taking my gun out. It's Amanda, looking peeved. I open the door. She looks nervous.

'Come in,' I say.

She walks in, carrying a small bag. 'I'm embarrassed to ask you this…'

'Don't worry. Spit it out,' I say.

'My room is flooded. Maintenance are in there working on it but it's too wet for me to return. And there are no other rooms available so I'm wondering whether I can sleep on one of your chairs.'

'No way,' I say and await her reaction.

'I guess I can sleep in my car or scout out another hotel in Katoomba,' Amanda says, 'I'm sorry to disturb you.'

'Don't be silly. You're staying here and sleeping in the bed. Have you seen the size of these beds? Big enough for a small family from a third world country.'

'You don't have to do that,' Amanda protests.

'But it's done. Have you had dinner?'

'Yes, but only a little plate to save your budget.'

'What's in the bag?'

'A change of underwear and tooth brush and cosmetics.'

'Very good,' I say, 'I have some overnight stuff in my car but I'll get it when the rain has stopped. Look, let's go to a bar for a drink and I want you to eat properly. They'll still have sandwiches at this hour I'm sure.'

We pop downstairs, enjoy a drink and a snack and chat about movies. It turns out we both enjoy a good thriller and we have a similar taste in books. When we are finished, I hand Amanda my key card and tell her I'll be up in a few minutes. I find an overnight bag which I keep in the car for emergencies and go back upstairs. The rain is light now and I expect to sleep soundly.

Curtains drawn, lights out, the darkness envelops us. Neither of us has night gear so we sleep in our underwear. But the bed is wide enough so that we both have sufficient room without touching each other.

But sometime in the early morning there is a thunder clap right above us and I'm woken by a body crashing into me. Amanda begins to apologise but I wrap my arms around her and tell her to hush, saying everything's okay.

She feels soft and incredibly sexy. I detect a swelling nudging my boxer shorts, realise it's the muscle of creation, and wonder what to do. She leans into me more and now I have a full-blown problem. I don't want to release her but know I must. I haven't slept with a woman since last Saturday night and I'm incredibly horny, but I have to control myself. She's half asleep and I don't want to take advantage of her. Not only could she inform the Police Department that she's been sexually harassed but worse she might say I raped her.

I try to think of a pleasant way out, a way which doesn't suggest I'm rejecting her nor saying I'm not interested, because I'm certainly interested, but I can't come up with a decent solution. Then I feel her lips on mine and this signals consent, doesn't it? I press my lips into hers and soon we're kissing passionately, the sounds of thunder obliterating any words which we may have uttered. Of course, I haven't spoken, and I don't during this kind of engagement, allowing the sensation of feeling flesh on flesh and my imagination to spirit me away. Towards oblivion. I'd thought previously that it's a shame that, after this kind of physical encounter, we return to the dreariness of ordinary life. But there it is, a momentary escape, be it two minutes or an hour.

Amanda wraps one leg over mine and I'm so far gone that I'm doomed. Nothing matters. They can send me away for a sexual crime or capital punishment. The sensation is electric, powerful, a moment I would give my life for. But then my senses return. I don't have protection, I realise. What if Amanda does this sort of thing regularly? And she has an STD? Not that I really think this, but the thought is enough to rescue me from being foolish. I break the embrace, whispering that we shouldn't.

She breaks off and we both lie, side by side, fingers touching. I hold my breath. How has she interpreted my move? I don't want to speak, to make what happened less than the magic it was.

'Thanks for bringing me back to my senses,' Amanda says, after another two minutes silence.

'Don't apologise. I very nearly did something from which I wouldn't be able to return,' I say in a soft voice. Then, 'Afraid of thunder?'

'The noise frightened me and it was so dark.'

'Come here. Let me give you a cuddle. Don't worry, I won't try anything. Besides I saw what you did with that Petrov woman.'

Amanda laughs then edges towards me and allows me to hold her, her back against my chest. My hand brushes her breasts and I note they are not too small nor too big. I lower my hands. I breathe. This is the second-best activity with rain pounding the outside.

We must have fallen asleep because when I wake, I see the digital time on my watch which is on the bedside table showing 7:47 a.m. I struggle out of bed and draw the curtains aside with the pulley. I see that Amanda is sleeping on her side.

'Oh, what's happened?' she asks.

'It's morning. Do you want to use the bathroom?'

'You go first.'

'I'll shower and get ready and you can doze a few more minutes.'

Ready for work, we wander downstairs and find a breakfast dining room.

After having some coffee, I ask, 'Sleep well?'

'I did. You?'

'Like a baby.'

'What's the plan for today?'

'I want you to talk to each of the five friends individually and record timelines. I know they gave us a rough idea of their times when they left the pool area but I'd like an exact time, to the best of their memory. I'm going to interview the Petrovs after talking to the Forensics team. Okay?'

'Yes sir…I mean Hank.'

'I hope you don't feel awkward on this job after last night. You don't have to continue if you feel compromised,' I say. As much as I'd like to work with Amanda, I'd replace her if she felt odd about being touched during the night. After all, nothing really happened. But these things can play differently in the mind for different people. For me, last night was last night and today is a new day and the past remains there, in the past. Admittedly I will remember the interaction with Amanda with fondness but I won't allow it to cloud what needs to be done on the job. I'm simply too professional.

'I'm fine. Last night was cosy but it won't affect work,' says Amanda.

'Good.' I'm happy I don't need to make changes.

NINE

HERB PETROV SITS BACK IN his chair in the interview room. He looks belligerent, no doubt unhappy about his accommodation for the night. And the fact he was separated from his wife would not have helped. I peer at him from an observation room and wonder how best to conduct the interrogation. I have a local cop to accompany me. He will be setting up the recording device. I nod at him and we proceed to the interview room.

Before coming to the station, I had an opportunity to talk to Samuel Ho, the Forensics team leader. He'd given me details of their search of the Petrov room and vehicle. He'd also advised that there were no prints on the knife stuck in Brent's neck. I hadn't expected anything else. Gloves were probably used in the attack.

DC Graham Hefferson and I sit opposite a surly Herb Petrov.

'Do you want legal representation?' I ask.

He shakes his head.

'Can you talk so that your response is recorded?' I stare at him to see whether he comprehends.

'No,' Petrov growls.

'Tell me what happened on the dance floor Friday night,' I say, brushing my short hair back with my right hand.

'I dance.'

'You also pushed another man and you were heard raising your voice.'

'Is this against law here? In Russia, there are fights and no cops come.'

'So why are you here and not in Russia?'

Petrov glares at me. 'I tourist.'

'And how are you finding it?' I ask, observing his snarl.

'Not so good,' he says. 'Rude people.'

'Is that why you later killed the man you'd pushed on the dance floor?'

'I kill no one. This is nonsense,' he says, raising his voice.

'Tell me what you did after you left the Boiler Room?' I stretch my leg a little.

Petrov explains in his best English that he and his wife left the dance floor near midnight and went to their room where they undressed and had sex. He says that dancing made his wife amorous. He says there were no witnesses to report that they went back to the hotel room. He insists that they should be released.

'Unfortunately we can't let you go Mr Petrov. Our team found significant quantities of ecstasy pills in your vehicle. So we're going to charge you for possession. And of course, resisting arrest.' I smile at him.

'I want lawyer,' he says.

'DC Hefferson will help you there. Thank you for your time.' I leave the room asking Hefferson to come outside for a moment.

'Would you check his wife's story to see whether there are inconsistencies?' I ask when we're outside the Katoomba Police Station.

'You've got it,' says the burly detective. 'I'll call you when it's done.'

'Thank you. I'd better get back to Medlow Bath,' I say. I shake his hand then walk to my car. I look back at the quaint building, two square slabs of brick divided by an entrance with a triangular roof peak over it.

Although I don't believe Petrov went back to kill Brent, as he displayed no knowledge of the pool and the cabins situated opposite the pool, I will question other guests to see whether Petrov's movements for the night in question can be verified.

When I arrive at the Hydro Majestic, I park the Commodore in a different spot and sit a moment, thinking about the murder case. I have no interest in the drugs matter and will leave the Katoomba police to deal with it.

I call Amanda before stepping out into the sunshine. It seems the storm has done its job and has left a clear sunny fresh day. She answers after a short wait.

'Hi,' she says.

'Where are you?'

'I'm in the Wintergarden and I'm working on the timelines.'

'See you in a moment.'

As I stroll into the hotel, I wonder which of the five friends I'm most inclined to distrust. It's my view that one of them is most likely to have performed the evil deed. Usually one suspects the spouse or partner, but all of these people might have had a reason to do Brent harm. We need to know more about them as the original enquiries only dealt with the circumstances of the period leading up to the murder. What needs to be determined is the motive. Each one of them had the opportunity.

I walk through one of the many colourful hotel corridors. Soon I'm in the Wintergarden and I see Amanda close to the window. I take a chair opposite her. She has an iPad open and she shows me that she has drawn up the timelines of the friends leaving Brent's cabin.

'What conclusion have you drawn?' I ask, looking at her bright eyes.

'None really. Each person claimed to have left well before two o'clock, the approximate time of death.'

'Do you think somebody who knew they were staying here could have come in late and carried out the crime?' I ask. This doesn't seem likely to me, but I'd like to get another view.

'That's doubtful. Who would have the need to do that? And how would they know where Brent was staying? Wouldn't it be much easier to kill Brent elsewhere, if a third party killed him?'

'I agree. Which means we need to explore each of the friends' lives further. Find out all about them. Tomorrow, I'll get data from the police databases about any criminal activity any of them may have been involved in.'

I grab a waiter's attention to get a cup of coffee. I don't expect we'll find the killer while we're here so, back in Sydney, I'll have more resources. I mention this to Amanda.

'Does this mean you won't require my services then?'

I examine Amanda's face. 'You'll still be part of the investigation. I'll talk to your boss to have you assigned to this case and to have you work out of headquarters in Parramatta.'

I review the information Amanda has collected and suggest we return to Sydney and recommence in the morning. 'You've done a fine job,' I say. 'If you email me the information you've collected, we'll have a closer look at it at Headquarters.'

'No joy with Mr Petrov?' Amanda asks.

'No Amanda. But we got him on drugs possession, assaulting police with a deadly weapon and resisting arrest. He held a large quantity of a variety of drugs. Katoomba will investigate whether he was going to distribute them.'

'I see. I guess we did the right thing then.'

More people are wandering into the Wintergarden and I don't want to talk about our cases. 'We should go. You have a few hours to enjoy the weekend.'

'Ok, Hank. I'll see you in the morning.'

TEN

I SEE THERE'S SOMETHING AMISS on my bank statement. I've brought in my mail this warm and overcast Monday morning but all I've been able to do is open the four envelopes and glance at the contents. Two bills, one donation request and my NAB bank statement.

I've come into the office early, arranged a meeting with my troops and informed them of what we needed on the five so-called friends of Brent Morton. Amanda attended, and I've given her the role of collecting the reports and co-ordinating results from five of my team assigned to scout out the lives of each of the friends. I've decided to look into Brent's background myself.

Meeting over, I'm free to delve into my personal affairs since I rarely get the time to manage paperwork, something I dislike intensely. But this withdrawal on my account is bothering me. Just as I'm about to call my bank, Amanda walks into my untidy office.

'Busy?' she asks.

'Did you get some non-interrupted sleep last night?' I look to see if she gets my meaning.

'I did, although I missed being held,' she says smiling. 'But there wasn't a thunder storm, so I managed okay.'

'Great. Want some help with anything? I take it my PA showed you where everything is?'

'Oh, yes, Claire's been helpful. I just want to know with whom I should speak to obtain the Forensic data?'

'Of course. Slipped my mind. Samuel Ho is the guy. Claire can direct you.'

"Thanks.' Amanda, who I notice is again dressed in dark colours, leaves.

I sit back and wonder what would have been had we proceeded to develop our physical relationship that night at the Hydro Majestic. A visit from Claire snaps me out of my day dream.

'Here's your coffee from down the road,' she says.

'Thanks Claire, you're an angel,' I say taking the carton from her.

'You know I should be doing work, not fetching coffee for you,' she says, smirking.

Claire is in her forties, a few years older than I am, but she's been my PA forever and she doesn't mind doing anything for me. But she needs to give me curry as well, part of our work dynamic. In return I look after her, come salary time and I also grant special requests from her when she has to take time off for her kids. She's also tried to set me up with women friends, but I've always declined the offer.

I sip coffee and refocus on my bank statement. Rather than wait on the phone for ages, only to get automated voices and people who have set routines, I decide to visit a local branch later this morning. I sit back again, enjoy my coffee and fantasize about Amanda. I've noticed how some of my male team members looked at her with longing and admiration. I didn't see what they saw immediately but then I was in the midst of witnessing a gruesome sight – a photo of Brent Morton's neck, knife protruding.

When I arrive at the bank, I ask to see a manager. I'm told a customer service specialist is available whereas the manager is presently occupied. As this is not a murder enquiry, I can't push the matter. I agree to see Mitzi Palmer who has an office on the side of the room. After a short wait, I'm invited in.

Mitzi is a pleasant looking short woman with the olive complexion of a Latin American. Unsurprisingly, she has jet black hair. She sits behind a desk with a desktop computer, the large flat screen to the side of the clean surface. When she speaks, I detect an accent from somewhere in South America. 'How can I be of assistance?' she asks, placing elbows on the desk.

'There's a withdrawal here which doesn't make sense. See what I've ringed,' I say, pushing the statement across the desk.

As Mitzi reviews the document, it occurs to me that she would have difficulty sticking a knife into a much taller man unless the man was sitting down. As I recall Brent must have been standing when the knife pierced the side of his neck, making it unlikely that Candice, also short, could have performed the deed. That would be the same scenario for Sally. However, Grant, Fiona and Mitch all had the ability to make the strike. Realising that, I will still consider each one of the friends as suspects until I can eliminate those with less motive than the others. Then height might become the definitive issue to clear them.

'I will look into this. It might take some time as I need to make some calls,' she says.

'I can't wait. Here's my card. Please call once you have the answer,' I say as I get to my feet.

'Okay. Oh, I see you're a detective,' says Mitzi, 'There better not be bad people involved.' She smiles as she holds out her hand.

'No,' I say, 'there better not.' I shake her small hand and leave.

Later that day, Amanda comes into the office again. She sits down, and I look up from a report I'm reading. It's a report on an ongoing case, a cold case about a murder committed a few years ago. 'Hi, what's going on?'

'I've seen Samuel and he has DNA and fingerprints from Brent Morton's cabin. I'll arrange for someone to take prints and DNA samples from the five friends,' says Amanda.

'Good. I should have a report back tomorrow from our electronic experts regarding their phones. See if there's anything that stands out, an argument with Brent or something sinister,' I say.

'When did you have their phones delivered to the electronics department?'

'I had somebody pick them up and pass them on. I wanted to have them examined quickly and Samuel was obliging, happy to work over the weekend.'

'You are a suspicious guy. I would never have thought of confiscating their phones so soon. What if they deleted texts beforehand?'

'No problem. Our team will be able to restore them.'

'Looks like you have everything under control,' says Amanda.

'Reports about the six friends will trickle through during the week. You should have all of them by Friday. Please read them and then come talk to me. I'd like your view of these people too,' I say.

'Okay boss.'

'By the way, our databases didn't come across any serious crimes from the five suspects. All except Fiona who had some traffic infringements. And Candice had one shop-lifting charge. That's it. Almost model citizens.'

'I see. Perhaps none of them killed Morton.'

'Perhaps. Talking of Morton, he did have two charges. One was for aggravated assault and the other was for affray at a party,' I straighten my posture, conscious that sitting too long in one position is bad for health.

'So, he was the most violent of the lot?'

'Appears that way.'

Amanda leaves. I wanted to ask her to join me for a drink at a pub after work but felt it was better to stick to best practice rules in the workplace. I may be foolish enough to kiss Amanda after a few drinks. It seems there's an increase in sexual assault complaints. The State Labour Opposition leader resigned recently for touching a journalist inappropriately. I can't afford to lose my job just yet.

ELEVEN

As I drive to Parramatta from my home in Collaroy, the sun is blazing, and I expect the weekend to be great. I might even have time to sneak in a game of tennis and a dip in the ocean.

Amanda informs me via intercom that she has the reports on the five surviving friends and we make an appointment to meet at 4:00 p.m. I ask her to email the reports to me, so we can discuss them at the meeting.

Max Dalton, a detective sergeant, comes into my office just before lunch. 'Doing anything for lunch?'

'Love to join you but I have reports which I have to read for a meeting. Next week might be better,' I say, stretching my arms above my head. I stand ready to leave the office to buy a sandwich from a nearby shop.

'Okay. Doing any fighting this weekend?'

'You mean UFC?'

'Yeah. You were going to invite me to your next fight,' Max says.

'I'll let you know when the next bout is,' I say.

Whilst having a ham and tomato sandwich, I review the first report sent to Amanda which she has now sent to me. It's about Mitch. It reads:

Mitch Norris is thirty-five years old and has a robust build. He grew up in country New South Wales. His parents are sheep farmers and still live in the country, on a farm south of Glenorie. His childhood was uneventful. He helped out on the farm, but it was clear he didn't want to continue in his father's footsteps. Besides he had an older brother who was keen to take over the management of the farm when the father retired. Mitch came to Sydney to take up a scholarship at the University of Sydney. He majored in computer science. He shared accommodation with four other students at a house near the university. One of the people in the shared accommodation was Brent Morton. The two men had a common interest in rugby union and they both played for the university's first team. Later Mitch switched codes and played rugby league for Manly.

Mitch was also keen on drinking and often went to pubs around the university with friends. He and Brent often went out together and occasionally got into fights after the pub's closing time. After Mitch's degree, he got a job in Sydney's CBD. He spent six years working for companies before starting his own business. He freelances for small businesses and individuals seeking computer solutions.

During his university years, Mitch met Sally, but they were only friends then. He kept in touch with Brent Morton, Sally McCarthy, Grant Michaels, Fiona Harrison and Candice Berry and they met on a day in November each year, a kind of anniversary. Mitch dated Sally after a reunion when he turned thirty. After two years dating, the couple married.

Mitch's friends describe him as happy-go-lucky, reliable and keen on football and golf. His neighbours describe him as fun. But one said he has a drinking problem and then he can be aggressive. He said he's heard the couple argue loudly at times.

There was only one occasion when Mitch and Brent were heard to argue. It happened one night after Brent was leaving Mitch's place and Mitch was heard saying that Brent was a bastard and that he never wanted to see him again.

But the next year, the six friends celebrated a weekend at a Port Stephens resort. We have no idea what the argument was about and how it was resolved.

I finish reading the report and sit back, threading fingers behind my head, to contemplate its value. Before getting on to the next report, I'm summoned by my boss. The meeting with him relates to a progress report on outstanding cases.

Back in my office I carry out administrative work and, when I've finished, I see it's almost four o'clock. As there's not much point getting into another report, I get coffee from the kitchen and wait for Amanda. She arrives promptly at four.

'Another coffee, I see,' says Amanda, taking a seat. 'You must live on the stuff.'

'It's not good to have too much. Is there such an organisation as CA, coffees anonymous?'

'I doubt it but who knows,' she says.

'Right, what did you think of Mitch Norris's bio?'

'Apart from that one incident when he argued with Brent outside his house, he doesn't seem to have a motive. The two seemed to have been close friends but until we understand what that argument was about, I can't say for sure he's out of the woods.'

'I tend to agree,' I say.

'Although he was so wasted on that night at the Hydro it's hard to imagine him being in a state to kill,' says Amanda, crossing her legs.

'He could have been faking if he intended to kill his so-called-mate.'

'True.'

I catch Amanda looking at me in a strange way. I wonder what it means. Is she waiting for me to invite her out? Or does it mean she's not really convinced about what I said of Mitch? I want to ask Amanda out for a drink but I'm still not sure. 'Have you had a chance to talk to Forensics to establish whether persons other than the friends had fingerprints in the cabin?'

'Yes, and it seems there are no prints or samples of DNA other than that of the friends. So, my idea of Petrov being a suspect was way off the mark,' says Amanda, recrossing her legs.

'Don't beat yourself up over it. It had to be explored. Also, if another party did do the deed, prints may have been erased.'

'Okay, which one next?'

'I haven't had a chance to read the others, so I thought I'd do it tomorrow and perhaps we could discuss them on Monday morning.'

Amanda says this as she gathers the reports she'd printed and placed on the side of my desk, 'Not a problem. About nine.'

'Absolutely. Enjoy your weekend…do you care for a drink before you head off?' I ask, conscious that I'm wandering into dangerous territory. I have no plan. Nothing. Just taking a risk. But I figure, she'll be here for only a short time and what have I got to lose? I'm been in precarious positions before confronting criminals and I've survived. I may not be so lucky the next time.

She hesitates, looks me in the eye. 'I'd love to.'

TWELVE

As I walk down to the Woolpack Hotel in George Street, Paramatta where I'd agree to meet Amanda, I contemplate my life. It began happily with two loving parents. As the only child, I was loved and well looked after until I turned twelve. Then a home invasion changed everything. Our Palm Beach home was invaded by two men who knew that my father, a jeweller, had a safe. They tied up my mother and forced my father to reveal the combination by beating him with a baseball bat. When the men first came in, I ran into the bathroom and hid there. I kept my ear to the door, and I heard everything. Then after the men got what they wanted they shot my parents, execution style. They were never apprehended. That was the inspiration for me becoming a cop. And I'm still working to find those monsters.

My aunt Jeanie who lived in Kirribilli took me in and raised me. My aunt's husband was a banker and made sure I was well educated by sending me to Sydney Grammar. I attended Sydney University and studied law. Then I joined the police department and became a detective after attending the police academy and serving as a policeman for six months.

I enjoyed my work and learnt as much as I could. I wanted to find my parents' killers, but I never mentioned to anyone that they had been murdered. I knew if I pursued an official investigation into their deaths, I'd be removed from the case because of a conflict of interest. But this didn't stop me from learning as much as I could from the files held on the data bases.

My love life suffered as a result of my determination to hunt down the killers. I couldn't commit to anyone so I generally only experienced short-term relationships. This hadn't bothered me as I'd not come across anyone with whom I wanted to settle down. I played the field, enjoyed female company but got cold feet when a couple of my girlfriends got closer, and wanted more than a fun time.

Somehow, I feel a little differently about Amanda and I can't put my finger on why that is. Why does she have a positive effect on me which isn't just sexual? It's puzzling. Perhaps if I saw her a few times, my usual abrasive self will return, and I'll scare her off. This meeting at the pub will be a test. Not only is a work-place romance risky but seeing somebody as a possible love-interest is also a gamble.

When I enter the pub, I find Amanda is waiting for me at a table. She's bought me a beer I see. She's nursing a gin and tonic. She smiles as I sit opposite her.

'Thanks for the beer. Sorry I'm late,' I say.

'That's okay. I understand a policeman's job is never done.'

'Spot on. Do you have cases waiting for you?'

'No, my desk is clear. The one case I was working on wasn't a big case, like murder, and somebody else is looking after it,' she says, sipping some clear liquid.

'Do you enjoy your work?' I ask, observing her closely.

'It has its ups and downs.'

'Why did you become a cop?'

Amanda smooths the front of her blouse. 'Wow, all the big questions.'

'Sorry, if you're uncomfortable talking about it, it's fine,' I say, wondering whether I've hit a nerve. Maybe she has a secret like I have.

'I don't mind talking about it. Only that it feels more like a job interview than a casual get-together to wind down after the week.'

'Yeah, I know I ask weird questions. Happens with my friends too.'

'You have friends?'

'Very funny. What would you like to talk about?'

'I'll tell you why I joined the police force. It's no big secret. I've always been keen to work out mysteries. Love cop shows on television and I just kind of fell into it when I figured I had nothing to lose. Didn't actually expect to get the job.'

'Right. Well, that's good. And murder cases allow you to solve the ultimate mysteries.'

'Why did you become a cop?'

I don't want to lie but equally I don't want to give away my real reason for becoming a detective. 'I did criminal law at university and thought I'd rather catch criminals than defend them.'

'That's a good explanation. I could see that you were committed to finding Brent's killer. More so than some colleagues who just see being in the police as a job, not a vocation.'

'Can I get you another drink?'

'Sure, I'm catching the train so I don't have to worry about driving, Can I have a gin please? I have enough tonic.' says Amanda.

I go to the bar and buy two drinks from a young tattooed bartender. When I return to the table, Amanda has disappeared. I sit down and scan the place. Busy now, being a Friday evening. I see a sign saying 'The smoother side of Jack' an advertisement for Jack Daniels. Being early, people are well behaved, many being office workers, enjoying a drink with colleagues. Trouble will tread water until much later, I suspect. A man in a suit and white business shirt asks whether he can take the unoccupied chair, but I shake my head.

Amanda returns. 'Getting crowded now,' she says, then thanks me for the drink.

'Where do you live?' I ask.

'Strathfield,' says Amanda.

'That's a decent commute to Penrith.'

'I manage,' she says. 'It's about 50 minutes to an hour.'

'Any plans for the weekend?'

'I'm going to the movies with a girlfriend Saturday night, otherwise I'll chill.'

'No boyfriend?'

'No. I broke up with a fellow seven months ago. Since then I haven't dated. Why are you interested?'

'Just curious,' I say, pleased she's available, but concerned this will tempt me to do something stupid.

'And you. A wife?'

I almost laughed. 'No wife, no partner or girlfriend. Free as a bird.'

Amanda smiles. 'Not interested in a relationship? You're getting on a bit in years, aren't you?'

'Yes, forty next month. I haven't found anybody who can put up with me,' I say which is almost the truth. I don't tell her I sometimes break things off with girlfriends if I haven't scared the women off after they get too serious.

'The long hours. I understand how the job can scare some women from committing, but you could go on a dating site and find somebody,' she says.

'Are you trying to be a match maker?'

She laughs. 'Not at all. Just offering a practical solution. Remember, I like to solve puzzles.'

We change the topic and talk about music and films. She likes comedies, police dramas and thrillers. At nine o'clock, Amanda says she'd better go home before she becomes too inebriated.

'Want a lift?' I ask.

'You shouldn't be driving,' she says.

'I haven't had that much over the time we've been here. Besides, you've been on spirits while I've had some beers.'

'Still.'

'You haven't answered my question?'

'If it's not out of your way?'

We drive to Strathfield and I stop outside her block of flats. I wonder whether she's going to invite me in but suspect it would be foolish for her and downright crazy if I were to accept. She slides out of the passenger seat, shuts the door and signals for me to lower the window which I do.

'Want to come in for a coffee?' she asks.

I nod. I kill the engine and we walk along the path in silence. The sexual tension is electric. One could spark a bushfire with it. Inside her second-floor flat, she reaches for the light switch but never gets to it. I take her in my arms, and we kiss like we're long-lost lovers, lips pressed together and moving. After a moment we pull apart. She finds the light switch then manoeuvres me into the bedroom. Luckily, she has protection in a drawer, but we're almost so engrossed with each other that we barely have time to apply it. The night passes in a flash, our bodies wasted in the morning.

THIRTEEN

AFTER SLIPPING OUT OF BED, I stretch, then hit the shower and dress. I leave the flat before Amanda wakes. I want to stay for breakfast, but I have work to do. When I get home, I change clothes and go to a nearby café for breakfast and coffee. I'm tired but I must read the reports and make notes. I don't want to spend Sunday working, if I can help it.

At home, I fire up my desktop computer and load the email from work. I lean back and for a moment indulge myself by thinking about the night before and about Amanda. I can't recall feeling as excited by anyone as I do about Amanda. I sip some water then attend to the business on hand. I read the report on Sally.

> *Sally McCarthy came to Australia with her Irish parents when she was six years old. She attended Macquarie University in the first year but transferred to Sydney University for the second year. She met Brent there. A couple of her friends alleged that she told them Brent raped her, and that she never reported it. However, through Brent, she met Mitch, Candice, Fiona and Grant.*
>
> *Sally became a high school teacher, taking English and History. She married Mitch and, according to Sally's mother, she wants children but so far that has been elusive. She's keen to obtain medical help but Mitch has so far refused to entertain the idea.*

Although Brent and Mitch were best friends, Sally had kept her distance from Brent, only occasionally going out with the two men as a foursome. Sally is nevertheless able to meet with the other friends on their annual meetings. According to her teaching colleagues, Sally is popular amongst staff and students. She's been involved in school productions and is known to volunteer time for the betterment of the school and pupils.

I sit back. Sally had a motive to kill Brent if the allegations are true. I make a note to follow up. I'd like to get her side of the story. Before continuing I call Amanda. 'You're awake,' I say when she answers in a groggy voice.

'Yes. What did you do to me?'

'You don't remember last night?'

'Of course, I do, silly. What time is it?'

'According to Northern Beaches time, it's eleven thirty,' I say, loving that she seems to be okay with the night and early morning.

'God, I've just got up. I'm starved. Why aren't you here to make me breakfast?'

'Cheeky bitch,' I say, 'I'd come over tonight and make you breakfast tomorrow morning, but you have a date with a girlfriend, as I recall.'

'Are you working through those reports? With coffee?'

'You've got it.'

'I need to get going,' she says, 'There's a knock at the door. I'll look forward to seeing you Monday.'

'See you.'

I refer to Candice Berry's report next. I recall an image of her. Big tits, small waist, large butt. Serious curves. Red hair.

Candice Berry is thirty-four years old and lives in Naremburn. She works in North Sydney as the leader of a claims section for an insurance company. She's been with the company for ten years. She went to Sydney University and did an Arts degree but she didn't finish it. She's active on Facebook and Instagram and has many friends. She's popular at work and seems to have dated a few guys from other sections at work. Her own team is comprised entirely of females. She talks about her love life to friends at work and we understand Brent had, in the past, forced himself on her. She didn't bother complaining to the police because of her association with the friends from university. She considers Fiona her closest friend. She's also been known to say she'd like Grant as a lover but it's never happened.

Candice's relationship with Brent was a torturous one. After university, Brent chased her. Flattered, Candice agreed to be his girlfriend. Apparently, he asked her to move in with him but she refused. Candice's neighbours claim they'd heard many noisy rows coming from Candice's flat. Candice also entertained other men at her place. Brent was a jealous man and had been heard threatening her.

It would seem that Candice had a colourful life except where Brent was concerned. He may have forced himself on her a number of times but she obviously accepted it as a price to be paid for acceptance with the university friends as Brent had introduced her to them. From interviews with colleagues and acquaintances, it appears Candice had a robust nature and didn't seem bothered with minor setbacks. She has a healthy level of self-esteem.

Her parents live in Victoria and they haven't been interviewed because they wouldn't know of her connection with Brent. Candice was not close to her folks and only spoke to them every now and then, according to what a close friend advised.

I get off the chair and walk to the window of my apartment, gazing at the ocean. The waves are gentle enough and I'm tempted to ditch what I'm doing to go for a swim. And that's what I do. It'll be good to exercise but also useful to consider the reports I've read. It would seem that Brent was not a decent human being and that a number of the friends had a motive to do him some harm. Killing him might be a little extreme but who knows what really transpired?

I wade into the water which is cold compared with the outside temperature. But after a moment I feel refreshed and I swim a short distance. The murder case disappears from my mind and I think how wonderful it would be for Amanda to be here, with me. To play. I swim back and forth for half an hour then get onto the sand which is now populated by those wanting to sun bake. I dry myself and walk back to my flat.

From the reports I've read to date, I believe follow-up interviews are needed. Nobody has expressed any concerns about Brent. What are they hiding, I wonder. When I get inside, I see a message on my phone, but I ignore it for now. I shower, allowing the warm water to flow over me. It feels great. When I emerge I feel like having a snooze. I do it, realising there's no rush to get through the reports.

I wake just after five o'clock. I wash my face with cold water and return to business.

FOURTEEN

I'm SITTING ON THE BALCONY and I watch the surf rolling in. I open my laptop and get it started, using a password which is different from the one I use on my work desktop computer.

Grant's report is the next one I read.

> *Grant Michaels is thirty-five years old and is a successful investment banker. He lives in a house in Watsons Bay. He owns two cars, a Porsche and a Toyota Rav4. Fiona Harrison moved in with him ten months ago. He is fashion conscious and always appears to wear what's in-style at any given moment. He loves to go shopping for clothes, cars, art work and electronics. He works hard, often putting in long hours. His colleagues say he's a perfectionist. He's not popular. He has great skills and wins clients through charm and intellect.*
>
> *Grant is close to his parents who live in Bondi. He visits them most Sundays for lunch. He bought them a house and a Toyota Camry. He is generous with those he cares for.*
>
> *Grant and Brent knew each other at Waverly Public high school, the only two who had a connection before university. Grant's parents were poor and couldn't afford sending him to a private school. Grant was bright however and gained a scholarship to study commerce and economics. He was one of the brightest university students of his year*

and was offered job opportunities from various quarters. He settled on Macquarie Bank which is an independent investment bank and financial services company. He impressed his bosses and rose steadily through the ranks. In only six years, he managed to become a top executive.

Although Grant and Brent have known each other the longest of all the friends, they rarely socialized other than at the annual meet ups of the university friends. This is probably due to the fact that they moved in different circles. After all, Grant was an executive in a top tier corporation and Brent ended up as a plumber.

Hence, we cannot glean from parents and friends and colleagues any known association with Brent. Grant's friends, other than the university group who have varied occupations, are all bankers, lawyers and accountants. He plays tennis and occasionally golf. He hates rugby and soccer.

Grant Michaels has had little time for romance and we only know of Fiona as a steady female companion.

After reading the report, I use the computer to check my personal emails and also surf some sites to catch up on the news. That done, I realise I'm hungry. I'm about to call Amanda to see whether she's still going to the movies when my phone buzzes.

'Hi there, it's Denise,' says a voice.

It takes me a moment for the voice and name to register but then I recall the woman I met in a bar last Saturday and we ended up at her place, fucking our brains out. "Hi, what's up?'

'I was wondering what you're up to. Are you free tonight?'

'Look, I'd love to get together, but I've been working today, and I'm still not done,' I say, wondering how she got my number. Was I so wasted that I didn't realise we'd traded numbers at some stage during the night? That's all I can put it down to.

'Why didn't you call me during the week?' Denise whines.

'I'm on a major case,' I say, 'You do know I'm a cop, don't you?'

'Oh, you never said. Sorry,' says Denise, sounding surprised. 'Maybe another time.'

'Sure,' I say. I disconnect.

I don't bother calling Amanda. I don't want to screw up somebody else's life. I get into the car and drive until I find a suitable place to eat. I have a steak with vegetables and a glass of red wine. During dinner, I consider Grant Michaels' report. It would seem he and Brent weren't really mates, and simply saw each other once a year. With little interaction between the two, it would appear, on the surface, that Michaels had no real motive for murder. But stranger things have happened.

I drive home from the Dee Why restaurant I've dined in, listening to music rather than thinking about the case.

My next report, which I decide to review in my study rather than going back onto the balcony, is of Fiona. The tall leggy blonde.

> *Fiona Harrison is thirty-five years old. She lives with Grant Michaels. The couple dated for a number of years before Grant invited her to share his large four bedroomed house, with swimming pool, tennis court and extensive gardens in Watsons Bay. Previously she had a flat in Newtown.*
>
> *Fiona, like Grant, is fashion conscious and we believe that's one reason why Grant became attracted to her. Fiona has had connections with Brent and close friends reveal Brent had had a few sexual liaisons with her whilst at university. But their relationship didn't last.*
>
> *Teachers and students found Fiona likeable but at times aloof. She works as a personal assistant to a partner in a law firm and is considered well organised and reliable. She is not prone to gossip so has few female friends at the company.*
>
> *Although Brent tried to date her after university, Fiona rejected his advances.*
>
> *Fiona likes to go shopping which seems to be her main non-work occupation. Often, she and Grant would spend Saturday afternoons wandering around shopping malls, browsing or buying clothes. They dine out often.*

After reading Fiona's report, I'm tired. I switch Netflix on my desktop computer and run through the offerings. I find some stand-up comedian and watch for half an hour before going to bed.

FIFTEEN

SUNDAY MORNING AND THE WEATHER is perfect for a run. It's not too hot, a breeze cooling the body. After my run I do some strength exercises on my self-arranged gym at home. I can't stand going to a public gym. Lack of time or interest, I'm not sure. But I go through the routines I'm comfortable with. Luckily, I had a sizeable inheritance from my father so that I could buy a property with views and one which had all the rooms and facilities custom made.

Now there's only one report left. Brent Morton, deceased. This report was constructed by Alex, someone I trust. I had intended doing the background on Brent but found myself tied up, so I outsourced it.

> *Brent Morton was thirty-five years and five months old when he died. He owned and operated a plumbing business which was not making much money. His finances indicated he had a large business loan to pay off. He also had a mortgage of $352, 700 owing on his property in Randwick.*
>
> *His customers had mixed opinions of him. Some said he did the job with no dramas, others said he was surly. But basically, nobody had a strong view one way or the other. He had few real friends, except for Mitch Norris. Females we interviewed who knew him didn't have a kind thing to say about him. He was a groper and someone with an exaggerated opinion of himself.*

> *He played rugby at university and played Rugby League for a local club. His teammates thought he was a good football player but a bad sport. He would drink too much on nights the footballers went out together and he'd start fights by inappropriately touching the girlfriends of other men.*
>
> *His parents live in Waverley but weren't available to talk. In conclusion, any number of people might have had it in for him.*

I sit back and lace my fingers behind my head. I wonder why Brent's parents hadn't told the investigator anything. Were they away or did they choose to be silent? Or perhaps they were grieving. I don't know the answer, but I will pursue this later.

Just as I'm about to go out to a pub, my phone vibrates. I'd put it on silent whilst I was working.

'Hello Mandy,' I say when I see the display.

'Mandy?'

'Isn't that your name?'

'If you'd like but please, not in the office,' she says.

'Of course not. How was the movie?'

'Good if you like the music of Queen.'

'I take it you do?'

'Of course, otherwise I wouldn't have gone.'

'That makes sense Ms Walsh,' I say, pleased to hear from Amanda.

'Just wanted to see how you're doing with the reports,' Amanda says.

'Checking up on me, are you?'

'I didn't want you unprepared for our meeting tomorrow.'

'I see. Why don't you come over and supervise in person,' I say, toying with her mind?

'I would but I'm visiting my folks this afternoon,' she says.

'See you in the office, Mandy. I did enjoy our time together,' I say, realising when I'd uttered the words that it's unusual for me to express my feelings so openly. Perhaps something is happening to me which I don't understand. Should I make an appointment with a shrink?

'I did too. See you. Bye,' she says.

* * *

I arrive in the office at 8:20 a.m. with a carton of coffee. I'm feeling upbeat as I'll see Amanda at nine. I'm wearing a dark blue suit with a freshly ironed pale blue shirt, black brogues and a red tie. I place my jacket on a hanger I keep in the office and return the hanger behind my door. I start up the computer and sip coffee while it does its thing.

At 8:55 my intercom buzzes. Who the hell, I wonder? My boss asks me to see him. As I wander out of my office, I see Amanda coming towards me.

'Won't be long,' I say, noting how beautiful she looks, her dark hair gleaming as though sunlight shines over it. 'Make yourself comfortable.'

Detective Inspector David Holtz ushers me to a chair in front of his desk. He is a tall balding man in his fifties with a round ruddy face.

'Rockwell, how are you?'

'Fine, sir,' I say wondering why he's enquiring about my health. Usually, he comes straight to the point, telling me what's happening or asking for an update.

He coughs as though he has something caught in his throat that he's trying to dislodge. 'Somebody from the station saw you Friday night with a female colleague at the pub.'

I want to ask who and whose business it is but hold fire. These days, we all have to appear politically correct. 'I had a drink with that female colleague.'

'Be aware that fraternisation with members of the opposite sex outside work is frowned upon,' he says.

I wonder whether that implies having homosexual connections is acceptable. Of course, that's not the case but I have to smile at the way these discussions must proceed. He should have just said fucking a colleague is out of bounds. 'Of course, sir, I'm aware.'

'Good. We don't want to have allegations of sexual misconduct arising out of the Murder Squad.'

'No sir, I'll be on my guard,' I say. 'Is that all, sir?' No doubt murder out of the Murder Squad would be likely to draw adverse criticism. But maybe not as much as sexual misconduct, as that seems to be the flavour of the times.

'Yes. How's that Blue Mountains murder case shaping?'

'Good, sir. We're making progress. I'll keep you informed.'

Holtz nods and I leave the office.

Amanda is seated and has her back to me when I enter my office again. I want to grab her and nuzzle her neck, not only because desire is flooding my body but also because I've been warned not to get involved with a woman at work. My rebellious streak is always high when I've been told off. I hate authority yet here I am, representing authority.

'Sorry about that,' I say, getting back into my swivel chair, 'the boss told me we were seen on Friday night and he warned me not to attract a sexual harassment claim.'

'I see. What would you do if I threatened to complain?'

'I'd have to kill you.'

Amanda laughs. 'That's what I thought.'

'Now, down to business. Let's talk about each one in turn. Your thoughts on Mitch Norris?'

'Apart from that loud and public argument with Brent, he was a close mate. But it depends what the argument was about, really,' Amanda says. She again looks at her notes. 'Not a strong contender.'

'I've come to a similar view. We need to talk to him and perhaps Sally about that. Why don't you take Sally and I'll talk to Mitch?'

'Shouldn't the two of us interview them together?'

'We could do that, but it'll take longer,' I say.

'Yes, I get it. Are you choosing Mitch because you don't want people to infer you might misbehave with Sally?'

'Do you trust me not to do something untoward with you?'

'Of course. I can take care of myself,' she says.

'Okay. Now let's talk about Sally,' I suggest.

'She has a strong motive, I feel. We probably need to confirm she was raped by Brent.'

'I agree. But being short kind of makes it not a strong case. I'm thinking of her height in relation to Brent's and the point at which he was stabbed. And she doesn't seem to be the violent type.'

'You don't know that. She might have stood on the bed. You see a petite woman and you think she's incapable. That's sexist,' says Amanda.

'Okay,' I say, not wishing to be drawn into a debate about sexism. 'We'll explore the rape angle.'

I make some notes on a small notepad. I stretch my arms and look at Amanda. 'What's that fragrance you're wearing today?'

'It's a Chanel Chance Eau de Toilette. Do you like it?'

'Not bad. Not that I'm an expert,' I say, wondering whether she usually wears it and I haven't noticed.

She smiles. 'Mind if I have a break. I'll get a tea. Do you want something?'

'No, I'm fine. While you're doing that, I'll organise meetings with Mitch and Sally, separately.'

When Amanda returns, I apologise and say something else has come up. 'I've arranged for us to see Sally at school at 3:15 p.m. and Mitch at his office at 2 p.m. I'll come by and we'll take a squad car.'

'Have you changed your mind about how to conduct the interviews?'

'Yes, I've considered your point and I agree it's best if we both see them. Okay with that?'

'Okay,' she says, taking her tea away again.

SIXTEEN

WE'RE SITTING IN A MEETING room in a Tech company in Chatswood, awaiting Mitch Norris to join us. It's a room with a long table and eight chairs and has glass surrounding it so everybody can see whether people are working or doing something devious, like flirting with the young women with heels floating by. I've seen a few young women wander past as Amanda and I wait for the IT manager, Mitch, to grace us with his presence.

I check the time. Mitch is already ten minutes late. I'm about to get up and force his hand when I see him striding towards us. I relax. He enters, and I note he's dressed in blue jeans, a khaki collared-shirt and runners. Not a fashion statement.

'Sorry detectives, had to sort out a crisis,' Mitch says as he enters the room and takes a seat opposite us. 'Need a drink. Coffee, water?'

'We're fine,' I say. 'We won't take up too much of your time. Just want to follow up on a few things.'

'Okay.' He leans forward.

'Who suggested the booking at the Hydro?'

'Jeez, I'm not sure. Either Fiona or Sally, they're the organised ones. I mean they like to make plans and bookings.'

'Do they book the annual gathering every year?' Amanda asks.

'Yeah. I think Grant did it once but usually it's one of the girls.'

I look at my notes. Mitch appears relaxed, arms stretched out on the table. Amanda knows from what I've done that this is her cue to ask the next question. We'd been over this on the ride to Chatswood where we'd found it difficult to get street parking. But we found a spot a block from this building.

'We understand that sometime recently you had a heated argument with Brent. Can you tell us what it was about?' Amanda's casual delivery takes Mitch off guard, but he seems to accept it as a fair question.

'I don't recall any heated argument,' he says.

'A neighbour said you'd followed Brent out into the front yard, and you told him you didn't want to see him again,' Amanda continues, while I watch the exchange.

'Oh that. Okay, I was angry with him, but we came to terms with it a few weeks later.'

'What was the argument about?' I ask, seeing that Mitch was going to slide right over it.

'Sally told me that he was coming on to her and I confronted him. At first, he denied it then Sally came into the room and she said he's lying. So, Brent fessed up but that made me really angry and I swore at him and basically told him to get out of our lives.'

'So why did you agree to see him again?' Amanda persists.

Mitch sits back and throws his hands up in the air. 'I cooled after a while. What was I going to do? He'd been my closest friend for over a decade.'

'But he made a pass at your wife,' Amanda says.

'Well, I spoke with Sally to find out what really happened. He wanted a hug and a kiss, she explained. What's the big deal, I thought.'

'Okay, thanks,' I say.

'Anything else?' Mitch is getting edgy.

'You and Brent got into some brawls when you went out to pubs and clubs,' I say, knowing about a couple but broadening the comment as I'm sure there were other occasions when the two of them caused trouble. 'Any comment?'

'We're…I mean, we were two high-spirited guys. After a day at sport, we were winding down and sometimes things would happen. But Brent and I never fought each other. We never engaged in a physical fight, if that's what you're getting at.'

'But you had physical altercations with others?' I ask.

'A few times maybe, nothing serious.'

'Of course not,' I say, standing. 'Thanks for your time.' I shake his hand, but he doesn't bother shaking hands with Amanda.

* * *

Sally is in a classroom when we encounter her. Another teacher told us where she would be. Today, Sally is dressed in a yellow dress, a belt around the waist. Her hair is pulled back to expose an open face with light freckles. She wears no make-up. Her shoes are flat making her seem even shorter than when she wears low or high heels. Amanda comments on this later as I was not aware of these details. We're asked to sit near her by bringing a couple of student chairs closer to her desk. The classroom seems to have enough furniture for forty students, and I wonder whether she actually teaches so many students, but I don't ask as I don't see the relevance. It's three-thirty and all the students have left.

We run through the same areas we had with Mitch except for the argument with Brent and her story is similar to his. She also confirms that she organised the latest best friends' meetings. She says that she and Fiona take turns in making the bookings and organising the attendees.

'What about Candice?' Amanda asks.

Sally laughs. 'She'd be a disaster. Totally disorganised is our Candy. But Grant did it once, if I recall.'

Finally, we run through the argument Brent had with Mitch. Sally sits and listens to what we heard from Mitch. When we finish, she says, 'Is that what he told you. Liar. Mitch likes to think I was exaggerating but Brent had touched me on the vagina. He wasn't hugging me; he was grabbing me.'

'Oh,' I say. 'We also heard from a friend of yours that Brent raped you when you were at university.'

'That's right, he did.'

'Why didn't you report it?' Amanda looks sympathetically at Sally.

'We'd been dating for a couple of weeks and when we were parked overlooking Bondi beach, Brent got frisky. Before I knew it, he was all over me. I wanted him to stop and I told him so, but he ignored me. Then later I realised if I said something, he'd say I was his girlfriend, and nobody would believe my story. So, I swallowed my pride, but I broke up with him before going out with him again.'

'How did he take that?' Amanda asks.

A male student enters the room, looks at us, then turns and leaves, letting the door slam. Amanda reminds Sally of the question.

'Brent didn't like it. Pursued me for weeks. It was a horrible time.'

'Did you ever tell Mitch about that incident?' I ask.

'No. I didn't want to sour Mitch's view of me,' Sally says. 'I know it sounds stupid now, in retrospect, but at the time I was going with Mitch, I just didn't think it was relevant.'

'So, you arranged the meeting at the Hydro where you knew the layout and the possible opportunity and then when the time was right, you returned to Brent's cabin and knifed him,' I suggest.

Sally looks shattered. 'No, no way. I didn't like the man, but I didn't kill him.'

'So, you say,' I say, 'Who can confirm your whereabouts?'

'Mitch,' she says.

'I thought you'd told us that he was incoherent and drunk.'

'I didn't kill anyone.' Sally looks close to tears.

Amanda and I wait for more. Sally remains quiet. She grabs a tissue from the box on the desk and blows her nose.

'We needed to make sure,' says Amanda in a placating tone.

'Okay,' says Sally.

We thank her and leave.

On the drive back to Headquarters, I ask Amanda whether she believes Sally's story.

'I do. She has a motive, a strong one, but she seems to think the rape was her fault,' says Amanda who is driving. I drove from Parramatta, but I let Amanda drive because I wanted to think clearly and not be distracted by traffic. Besides, I hate the peak-hour traffic at all times, but particularly from the city to Parramatta.

'You're probably right but, as far as I'm concerned, I'm not ready to eliminate her as a potential suspect. She organised the outing. She had reason, although it may have been buried in her subconscious mind. She doesn't have an alibi because Mitch was supposedly too drunk to notice if she went back to Brent's cabin.'

'But she's too short,' Amanda offers.

'Of course, why didn't I think of that? Short people don't kill.'

Amanda laughs. 'You're an idiot,' she says.

'It's why you like me,' I say.

'Since when did you think I liked you?'

'Good point. Watch the road.'

Back in my office, we review the other reports and plan our strategy for the next day.

SEVENTEEN

WHEN I WALK OUT OF the front door, Tuesday morning, after having been for a run, I'm wearing a suit again but it's far too hot for that. Today, the temperature, this early in the morning is thirty degrees or more and the day will only get hotter. I take my jacket off and wait for the Uber. As I live in Collaroy, I have no intention of going into Headquarters. I will Uber to see Candice in North Sydney. I've also asked Amanda to take the train there and we've agreed to meet at a café. Without my morning coffee hit, I'll be fairly useless at the interview.

Amanda arrives just as I take a seat in the café in Mount Street. 'How do you know this place?' Amanda asks.

'I've been around,' I say.

'Have you had breakfast?'

'Cereal but no coffee. You?'

'I didn't have time. Woke up too late. I might order a muffin.'

'I'll get it, you stay here.'

When I take my seat, I can tell that Amanda is worried about something. She looks tired and doesn't have that bright-eyed expression I'm used to seeing. I decide not to enquire. I'd like to but I don't feel close enough to her yet. Having slept with her once doesn't mean I can intrude on her emotional state. Unless, of course, it's detrimental to the job. But I don't need to ask her anything. Once the coffees and muffin are delivered, she leans over and speaks.

'Last night I had a visit from my ex-boyfriend. He wants to get back with me again and we talked through most of the night, but we didn't sleep together,' she says.

I'm surprised to feel put out, like I've been punched in the gut. But I don't show any emotion. I keep my facial expression neutral. This is why she looks wrung out. But why did she tell me she didn't sleep with him? Does she still want to see me? I ask, 'Do you want to get back with him?'

'I don't know. We've had a relationship which lasted five years. I thought we were going to get married. I'm still confused. Sorry to burden you with this but ever since that night at the Hydro, I've been thinking about you,' she says. She digs into her blueberry muffin, taking a huge chunk out of it.

I sip my Cappuccino. As much as I want but can't have Amanda, I don't like to see her miserable and that's how she appears at this moment. I'm just going to have to accept that my love life is always going to be not what I'd like it to be. To me, love is a greater puzzle than a homicide. Most murders are predictable and solvable. Love cannot be solved. It's mysterious, much like the universe itself. To deal with this, I resort to my stock-in-trade: flippancy. 'Well, you're on the right track. Think of me and nothing else.'

Amanda tears up. I place my hand over hers. 'Sorry, I'm only kidding. It'll sort itself out. Just don't let it get to you. Your heart will decide what's best for you and then it will work out. Thinking about this will drive you crazy. Now, finish your breakfast as our appointment with Ms Berry is due in ten minutes.'

She finishes her blueberry muffin.

* * *

Candice Berry is in the conference room as Amanda and I walk in. She looks as delicious as ever. Gazing at her superb curvaceous figure, all my concerns with Amanda disappear. I'm shallow, so shallow. It only takes a beautiful woman to set my mood to upbeat. I take Candice's outstretched hand and hold it for a fraction too long. If only I could bury my face between her large breasts? That would make my life wonderful again. Amanda has disappointed me and I'm hurting so I need some soothing, I feel. But first, to murder.

'Lovely to see you again, Candy,' I say, 'we won't take up too much of your time.' This is a statement I make time and time again, but I don't believe a word of it. The interview will take however long it takes.

Amanda nods at Candice and we all sit down.

'How can I help?' Candice asks.

'Brent,' I say, 'you had a relationship with him, we learned. Why did you end it, particularly as he gave you a lift to Medlow Bath?'

Candice pushes her hand with long red fingernails through her red hair, some of which has fallen across her forehead. 'It didn't work between us. We had a brief relationship after university, only for a few months, I think.'

'Who ended it?' asks Amanda.

'I did,' says Candice.

'Was there anything in particular which made you do this?' I ask.

'He was too rough. I didn't like the way he treated me.'

'Rough sex or being pushed around and hit?' Amanda enquires.

'No, nothing like that. He is uneducated. Talks rough and treats people with little respect.'

'But physically, he was okay?' Amanda asks.

We wait. When Candice doesn't expand on her response, I ask, 'Was it true he raped you at university?'

'Yes. Well he forced himself on me. Other boys did too but I managed to tell them to stop and they did. But Brent had no control.'

'So why did you get into a relationship with him later?' Amanda is letting this get emotional, her tone suggesting she cannot understand the woman's rationale.

'I can see how you would come to this conclusion, but I thought he might have changed. He seemed more mature when we met again, through the friend's annual get togethers. And I thought he was sweet when he invited me out and brought flowers. For the first few weeks, he acted like he was reformed, and I imagined his earlier behaviour was due to him sowing his wild oats. But it didn't last. He was abusive and controlling and he thought he had the right to have sex whenever he wanted.'

'Did you think of reporting this to the police?' I ask. I feel sorry for Candice. I could understand how men would have chased her and wanted her, but this torment was something I never imagined a woman would have to endure.

'What good would that have done? I'd read of women getting AVOs which have turned out to be useless. And the police would say they couldn't do anything unless they had proof of physical abuse. Which I didn't have.'

'Yet you were prepared to meet with him at the Hydro,' Amanda says.

'Only for the convenience of the ride. I told him to keep away from me once we were up there,' says Candice.

'You would have been happy to see him dead,' I pose.

'If I'm honest, yes. But I didn't kill him.'

Having heard what Candice had gone through, I say, 'Thanks for your time.' I stand, and Amanda does too. I shake Candice's hand again. In one way, I hope Candice is not guilty of Brent's murder. She's gone through enough with the bastard. If he were still alive and I knew of her torment, I would gladly give him a hiding he wouldn't forget.

Our next appointment is with Grant Michaels, the big-time investment banker. He's agreed to meet up at a city café. Being a senior executive, he can make time whenever he wants for personal errands. He probably doesn't want anyone in the firm knowing that he's being interviewed by the police.

Amanda and I arrive In Martin Place at 11 a.m., as scheduled, then wait for Grant on the corner of Pitt Street and Martin Place. As we watch people drift past, office workers stretching their legs, out for coffee or simply bludging, I say to Amanda, 'Do you think Candice could have murdered Brent? I don't think she's a likely candidate.'

'Why? Because you like her. Were you aware you were almost panting in the interview? I thought your eyes were going to pop out of your head,' says Amanda, looking at me strangely.

'Wow, back up. I was trying to take a more softly, softly approach as you and others sometimes think I'm too aggressive. Was I really that bad?' I'm sure Amanda sees right through me. I should be ashamed of my behaviour but I'm not. Besides, Amanda is going to desert me, and I haven't come to grips with that yet.

'About Candice...,' Amanda says but she stops when we see Grant striding towards us.

'Hi there, you two,' Grant says, 'Follow me and I'll shout you to the best coffee in the city.'

After ten minutes we're underground off Martin Place and Grant orders coffee for all of us. He doesn't bother asking whether we'd prefer something else. 'Now, how can I help?'

Grant is dressed in a grey suit which I estimate would have cost more than my entire wardrobe. He also walks in polished black leather shoes from which you could eat food and wears a white shirt with a red collar so firmly pressed one would wonder whether it's dry cleaned every hour. He oozes charm and I see that Amanda is flattered by his attention and direct gaze. He barely acknowledges me and that's going to bite him in the arse.

'You've never liked Brent, have you?' I ask, to kick off proceedings. The area here is spacious and has room for many eateries.

'Why do you say that?' Grant has to turn his attention towards me by looking directly into my eyes, a give-away sign. It means he's being honest or evasive. I'm not quite sure which yet.

'You've known him longer than any of your other friends, yet you don't mix with him socially except for the annual get togethers,' I say.

Amanda sits bemused, no doubt wondering why I'm being so aggressive, particularly after our discussion regarding Candice. I also don't like this trumped up high-flyer. He's so well turned out, I have to wonder if he's gay.

'We're different, that's all. We get on when we meet each year. We also live in different areas and have different interests. Simply, not much in common.' Grant sits back as the coffees arrive. He has also ordered some cakes.

Amanda takes a piece of cake and I see her eyes light up. 'This is delicious,' she says.

'I'm glad you like it. Made with natural ingredients. Nothing artificial at all,' says Grant.

The two chat about natural foods and I wonder whether they want to be left alone. If I leave, they probably wouldn't even miss me.

'How long have you known Brent?' Amanda asks, probably more to be friendly than to refocus on the case.

'Since primary school. He was in my class,' Grant says.

'Did you play sport together?' I enquire.

'He liked football and I liked chess so, no.'

'How did the six of you become friends then. It seems to me that none of you have much in common except for your annual meet ups.'

'I grant you it seems like that,' says Grant, 'let me tell you how it happened.'

Amanda finishes her second small cake and looks up, interested. I sip my coffee and wait for this revelation.

'The one class at university we all had in common was History. One day towards the end of the first year the lecturer thought it would be good to go on a tour to learn about history first-hand. A tour to Europe and places where the world wars were fought. The six of us were the only ones keen to go. So, we signed up, paid our funds, and undertook the excursion. As you can imagine, during that month-long tour, we went out most nights, drinking and socializing. We had a great time, and we got to know each other like family.'

'Wonderful,' Amanda says.

To get back on track, I say, 'So you didn't mix with Brent other than at the annual meetups, is that right?'

'That's correct.'

'Did you get into an argument with Brent on the Saturday night you all went skinny dipping?'

'No.'

After a little more general talk, we thank Grant and leave.

* * *

Amanda and I walk to the Wintergarden in O'Connell Street in the blazing sunshine. I make a comment that the day is too nice to spend working and that we should be at the beach.

'Too right,' Amanda says. 'For you, the beach is only a short walk away, is that right?'

'Yes. You should come over,' I say, forgetting that Amanda has another bloke now.

'I'd love to but until I sort out my life, I can't.'

'Of course. I wasn't thinking. Let's have lunch.'

We grab some take-away food in the food court in the Wintergarden then wander down to Bligh Street and the offices of Clayton Utz, lawyers. We ask for Fiona and she comes to greet us and ushers us into a private meeting room. She looks elegant in a beige suit which shows how leggy she is. Unfortunately for me, her legs are covered.

Seated, I tell her the usual spiel about the need for a brief follow up and that we won't take up too much of her time. Then I ask, 'Do you know anybody who would want to harm Brent?'

'Probably easier to tell you who wouldn't want to harm him,' she says which takes both Amanda and me by surprise.

'You included?'

'Oh yes. He was a wretched human being,' she says.

'In what way Fiona,' says Amanda.

'He rubbed everyone up the wrong way, with the exception of Mitch. Grant didn't have a kind word to say about him. And Sally and Candice hated him although they kept their feelings about him to themselves when he was around. But, in private, they trashed him. And as I told you before, he virtually raped me. To be fair I should have pushed him off me, but I felt powerless so I'm to blame.'

'You're not to blame,' I say. 'So, is he so repulsive that you knifed him? It's better if you tell us the truth. Did he try to force himself on you at the Hydro and you killed him in self-defence?'

'Ha ha. No such luck. I don't know who killed him, but it wasn't me,' says Fiona, taking the water jug from the centre of the table and pouring some into a glass. She looks at us to see whether we want some.

'No thanks,' I say. Then I add, 'It seems all you females had a motive to kill him. He seems to have forced all of you to accept his sexual advances.'

'I can't speak for Candice or Sally, but I got over him and didn't see the need for revenge years later.'

We end the meeting soon after and Amanda and I step outside into the heat, compared to the cool air-conditioned office. I hail a cab and we slide into the back seat. I inform the driver where to go and smile at Amanda. 'Beautiful day," I say.

As I don't wish to discuss the case whilst we're in the cab, we ride in near silence to Headquarters, with only the occasional comment about something innocuous.

Back in my office, I ask Amanda what she thought of Fiona's statement.

'She didn't like Brent, did she? But I can't see her killing him,' she says.

'All the women have motive and as an extension, the men do too, in support of their females,' I say, 'So we can't rule anybody out.'

'I agree,' says Amanda.

'We're back to square one,' I say.

'From what Fiona said though, if Brent had the personality to infuriate friends, he may have had some real enemies.'

'That's right. We should meet with Brent's parents and get a fix on the guy,' I say.

'Okay. Do you want me to make an appointment?'

'That'll be great. Tomorrow or the next day. Find out if they work and where and let's see them separately, if at all possible.'

'Will do boss,' says Amanda who leaves my office.

Seeing her depart makes me feel sad that there's another man in her life. But then, life doesn't work out the way one expects.

Thinking about the upcoming weekend, I feel disenchanted with going to a club and picking up a woman. Generally, apart from sex, none of the women I've managed to take home have turned out suitable for a longer-term relationship. I'll have to consider other avenues to meet a partner.

When I get home, I wonder whether using a dating site, something I've always avoided, would work for me. Using Google, I check out possibilities.

EIGHTEEN

Mr and Mrs Morton live in a small house in Waverley. The brick veneer structure has virtually no front yard. Standing in front of the door, this warm Wednesday morning, but cooler than the day before, I wink at Amanda then use the door knocker to register our arrival. Mrs Morton agreed to see us at ten-thirty. We are ten minutes late due to the difficulty in finding a parking spot, though Amanda eventually found a spot in a side street. But will we find it again later? I don't pay much attention at times and today I was consumed with how to discuss why somebody would want her son dead, realising it would be a sensitive issue.

We wait, and I check the time on my iPhone. Is she punishing us because we're tardy? I'm about to knock again when the door opens, and a smiling woman checks our identification before letting us in. Mrs Morton is around sixty years old, I guess, but she seems agile and fit. Well dressed in a polka dot dress and comfortable grey shoes, she invites us to take a seat at the kitchen table. Obviously, this is no social occasion for her. She doesn't offer us tea, coffee or water and that's fine with me.

'I'm sorry for your loss Mrs Morton,' I say, glancing at Amanda to check I've said the right words.

'Thank you,' says Mrs Morton, wringing her hands. 'Please call me Grace. How can I help you? I don't suppose you've caught the killer.'

'Sadly, no,' I say. 'We'd like to know more about Brent, particularly to understand who may gain from his death.'

Grace Morton places her hands on the table, and I see she has jewellery on fingers of both hands. She draws in breath before speaking. 'Brent was a difficult child, I understand. I'm not his natural mother. My husband Ken divorced his wife who was a lush and he got custody. Since I've known Brent, he's had problems with mixing in. He only had one real friend as far as I can tell, Mitch Norris. I don't recall anyone who hated Brent, but I know he can be a pain sometimes.'

'What about girlfriends?' Amanda asks.

Grace looks directly at Amanda. 'He never had a steady for long, love. That might have contributed to his attitude. He was a needy lad. Even as an adult, I didn't think he was mature for his age. Don't tell his father that. The two of them watched footy on the TV most weekends and they're close.'

'Where is Mr Morton now?' I ask.

'He works at a panel beating place in Bondi Road. He'll be home around six if he doesn't go to the pub,' says Grace.

'Can't help admiring that ring on your right hand. Ruby, isn't it?' I ask.

'Yes, it's a debutante ruby and diamond ring. I shouldn't be wearing it around the house, but I love it so much,' she says, touching it with affection.

'Must be worth something,' Amanda says, 'It's lovely.'

'Yes. Many thousands.'

'Where did you buy it?' I ask, watching Grace closely.

'Ken gave it to me as a gift before we were married. Why are you so interested?'

I smile at her. 'My father was a jeweller, so I made a point of learning about the trade.'

'Anything else?' asks Grace.

'No enemies that you can think of then?' I persist.

'No,' she says, a little too emphatically.

'You said he had only one friend. What about Grant, Fiona, Candice and Sally?'

'I know he went on excursions with a group every year, but Mitch was the only one who ever visited Brent or went out with him. Perhaps they met up at the pub occasionally.'

'He still lived here, did he? This is the address on his driver's licence,' I add.

'Yes.'

We thank Grace Morton for her time and leave, giving her our business cards as we'd done with all the people we'd interviewed. This is a tradition. I'm not sure whether anyone ever calls to provide additional information, but I abide by the ritual, nonetheless.

Walking to our Ford squad car, I feel a slight breeze which is invigorating after sitting in that stuffy kitchen with the latent bacon smells. The inside of the house was old fashioned, but tidy. I wonder whether Grace made it tidy before our visit. That was something my mother would do whenever we were entertaining or even if she knew of visitors coming, such as doctors or insurance salesmen.

'You showed a lot of interest in that ruby,' says Amanda.

'Just a polite enquiry,' I lie.

'Why didn't you ask about the other rings she wore?'

'I don't know.'

After some missteps, taking a couple of wrong side streets, we arrive at the car. I let Amanda take the driver's side.

'When are we seeing Ken Morton?' I ask.

'At his lunch break, around noon,' says Amanda, switching on the ignition.

'Don't you think it odd that a man in his thirties still lives, in Brent's case lived, with his parents?' I say.

'He was obviously a loner, not able to connect with people like others,' Amanda replies.

I don't continue the discussion. For our purposes, it makes no difference where he lived. 'We're near Bondi Beach. Let's look at the waves until we need to see Mr Morton. It's eleven-twenty now,' I say, not wanting to waste the morning by just sitting parked in a street.

Amanda drives down Bondi Road and parks the car facing the beach. We both sit back and watch the activity. Surfers paddle up and down and occasionally catch a wave. There are also people in the water, cooling down. Maybe they're tourists or people who are on holiday or sick leave.

'Nice spot,' says Amanda.

'Not bad,' I say. 'I prefer the Northern Beaches. Bondi is over-crowded.' Then after a moment gazing at the ocean, I change the topic, 'What have you planned for this weekend?'

'Not really sure,' Amanda says, 'First I need to sort out the mess which is my love life.'

We sit in silence for a few moments. I can't comment about Amanda's dilemma and will remain quiet on that. I look up at the sky. 'The universe is vast. We are insignificant really. So why do we torment ourselves during our brief time here?' I don't know whether Amanda is religious so I'm keen for her response.

'You're right, the whole subject is fascinating. But I rarely consider it. I'm busy enough managing the day to day rather than trying to figure out the mysteries of the universe.'

'Sensible way to go. I'm interested in dark matter, the expansion of the universe which scientists believe is happening and whether other intelligent life is out there,' I say.

'I didn't pick you as a deep thinker,' says Amanda.

I slap her thigh. 'Nice,' I say, 'you thought I was the proverbial plod, did you?'

'Of course not, but I am finding you more and more interesting the more I get to know you.'

'Really. That surprises me.' I grin. I'd like to move across and kiss Amanda but resist. It wouldn't be the right thing to do on a job.

'What's the time?' Amanda asks.

'Time to meet Mr Morton.'

* * *

The panel beater shop has broken cars all around, bruised metal, smashed in car fenders and rears. The cars which are too damaged don't make it here. They're write offs and taken to the car morgue where they are crushed for scrap metal. We walk into the main area of the shop which has vehicles being worked on by a number of panel beaters and I ask the first guy I see for Ken Morton.

'You are?' a man in dirty overalls asks. He has a big belly and a ruddy face.

'I'm DS Hank Rockwell. We have an appointment.'

'Kenny,' the man shouts, 'people to see you.'

Amanda looks around, I observe, with some distaste. After a moment, a man with a broad build but a few inches shorter than I am, strolls across, wiping his hands on a grimy rag. 'Yes, mate, what do you want?'

"I'm DS Rock…'

'I know who you are. Coppers. What are you after?'

Amanda steps in just as I'm about to make an unkind remark. Already I don't like this man and I wouldn't trust a word which oozes out of his mouth. He's probably been in trouble with the police before and, as a result, carries a grudge. 'We'd like a word about your son. Let me say we're sorry for your loss.'

'Don't bullshit me,' Morton says, 'you couldn't care less.'

I'm sick of this. 'Do you have somewhere private where we can talk?'

'Hah, mate, ask what you have to here,' he says.

I look at the man. He has salt and pepper hair and a snarl for an expression. He doesn't want to talk, that much is obvious. 'Right then, you're not interested in us tracking the killer. Your loss,' I say, turning around and walking away.

'Hey, hey, I loved my boy,' he says marching to catch up. 'There's a place outside here.' He leads us to a little indent at the back of the Panel Beater's structure.

We ask the questions relating to Brent's friends and enemies and don't find out much extra from him as compared to Grace Morton's comments. I let Amanda handle most of the questions which allows me to watch Ken Morton's facial tics.

As Amanda runs out of questions, I say, 'Tell us what sort of son he was.'

'He was a great guy. Loved footy, a beer and the beach. Was out a lot. Don't know what he got up to. He was over 21. No need to keep tabs on him.'

'Right.' I realise we're not going to get anything useful from Morton. I glance at Amanda.

We leave after Amanda thanks Morton for his time.

As we walk back to the vehicle, something bothers me. I don't know what it is. Amanda breaks into my thoughts. 'He didn't add anything useful, did he? What do you think?'

'I agree. But we had to try.'

Only later, when I'm at home, having a shower, the misgiving I had comes to me. The voice of Ken Morton. I've heard it before. And coupled with the ruby on Grace Morton's right hand, I realise that it may have been Ken Morton who broke into our house all those years ago and stole the jewels and executed my parents. At least that's what I believe. Could I be wrong? It was such a long time ago.

I ponder this as I dry off. Do I think this because I don't like the man? Or is my imagination running wild? I dress and grab a bottle of Peroni out of the fridge, sit outside on the balcony and close my eyes. I try to think back to that time when I was hiding in the bathroom, listening to the activities in the living room of my parent's house.

Then a revelation comes to me.

I'm certain I'm right about this and a buzz of excitement runs through me. I stand up and swing my arms about, exercising them. I'm so hyped that I want to take a woman, preferably Amanda, and drive my spear into her.

NINETEEN

Amanda peers into her fridge. She doesn't have much food in here, but she'll be able to make something with the chops, potatoes, carrots and peas. Vegetables are important, and she'd skipped cooking anything substantial over the past week. Her work, Jason's sudden emergence and being away in the Blue Mountains put paid to that.

As she cuts up the vegetables, she reflects on the day. She finds Hank fascinating but scary. His interest in bizarre subjects at odds with each other: astronomy and jewellery. But then he was such a surprise at the Hydro Majestic and the night they spent together. She'd never have guessed he could be such a thoughtful and skilled lover. But thinking about Hank is foolish, she realises, because Jason has come back into her life. However, she can't help it. The memory of Hank will linger.

She puts two lamb chops into a hot pan and the meat sizzles. A knock on the door snaps her out of her thoughts about Hank Rockwell and how she would like to form a relationship with him. But this wouldn't be feasible, given he's a colleague and the association would be frowned upon.

She runs to the door and opens it. Jason stands there smiling with a bunch of flowers in his hand. He passes them over. Amanda takes them and says, she is in the middle of cooking, so he'd better come in. As she continues with preparing her meal, she finds herself being annoyed with Jason. He hadn't called, just took it upon himself to come over.

'What're you making?' asks Jason, standing behind her in the small kitchen.

'Would you like some?' Amanda asks. She knows she doesn't have enough for two right now.

Sure,' says Jason who puts his hands on her shoulders.

Amanda freezes at his touch. She doesn't know why. She moves away to get more chops. She glances at him and finds his smug expression irritating. Although they'd talked about many things the other night, about the past, why they'd separated, they didn't get physical. But now Jason appears to think, it's acceptable to act like they are still together. Amanda wants time to understand her conflicting feelings.

They eat without much conversation and Amanda sees that not much will change. When they were previously in a relationship and once the early euphoria had dissipated, there wasn't much communication. They had simply got together for sex or going out with friends. Now, when Amanda looks back on their time together, she sees how unhappy she was with that scenario.

After dinner, Jason suggests going out for a drink.

'No thanks,' says Amanda, 'I have a murder enquiry going on and I'd rather be sharp for that.'

'Oh, come on, don't be so boring.'

'Sorry. It's my first murder case and I don't want to wreck the opportunity to do more real detective work.'

'Jesus, don't be so dramatic. You're a cop and you'll find you get to do what the higher ups want. It's just like being in the public service. And I should know. I've been working in Government for nearly ten years now.'

Amanda, at that moment, knew it wasn't going to work out with Jason. 'Alright, think what you like but I'm going to bed, alone.'

Jason walks out of the flat, slamming the door.

In bed, Amanda continues to read her book, a crime fiction tale by J.D. Robb in which the female detective is in love with her partner who surprises her because of his affection for her. When she puts it down, she turns off the light, closes her eyes and thinks about Hank, a man whose sometimes abrasive nature can switch to being adorable.

* * *

I wake Thursday morning, feeling inspired. After changing into running gear and brushing my teeth, I go outside and see the day is partially cloudy, huge white blobs floating across the sky. The temperature feels just right for a run.

During my jog along the beach, I try to figure out how I can find Ken Morton's partner in crime. Obviously, I can't simply ask him. Also, this is a private matter, so I can't use police resources to tail him. But I'm not discouraged as I feel I'll work out an acceptable solution in due course. In the meantime, I need to focus on Brent Morton's murder. It's ironic that I should be getting justice for my father's killer's son. I smile at the thought.

Back in the office, I schedule a meeting of my team, people involved in the case at one time or another. Amanda enters the room, coffees in her hand. She deposits a carton on my desk.

'Thank you,' I say, 'What's this for?'

'I know you like coffee and it helps put you in a good frame of mind,' says Amanda.

'Why do you want me in a good frame of mind? Do you need some time off?' I ask, intrigued. I sense Amanda is in a lighter mood and I love to tease her.

'No. Just keen to continue the work.'

'That's great. As you know, we're meeting in the conference room at 11 a.m. Bring along your notes and ideas. Thanks again for the coffee.'

Just after eleven, I arrive in the large conference room and see that the team has assembled. Apart from Amanda, I see that Rita and Jackie are seated in the front. Alex, Joe, Nick and Frederick are scattered further back. 'Hello everyone, thanks for coming in so promptly. I know you have plenty of work so I won't keep you long. You've helped with the Morton murder and I'd like to hear your take on it and any theories you might have.' I sit down and relax. I'm always keen to listen to fresh ideas.

Alex, a young keen detective begins. He is six-foot tall, sports a closely trimmed beard, and wears black jeans and a dark collared shirt. 'Lack of concrete evidence is the real problem. Prints from the victim's cabin confirm that all members had been in there on the night in question. We found a few other prints, but they led nowhere when we examined our data bases. From the summaries you've sent us, I figure it's one of the friends who did the deed and my guess is that Candice, although she has played down the rape, is the killer.'

This brought some noise with a rowdy debate ensuing.

'Quiet please. You'll all get a chance. Who's next?'

Jackie, a dark-haired slim woman of thirty-two years old with olive skin, puts her hand up. 'All the women have strong motives, so I'd re-examine their stories. Mitch was a best mate and too drunk on the night and Grant seems highly unlikely as a suspect.'

'Have we considered Herb Petrov?' Frederick, a usually self-contained man of forty-six, queries. Frederick is short and wide and hasn't enjoyed being out in the field. His forte is the thorough analysis of data presented to him by others.

'We have looked into his likelihood of being the killer, but he was eliminated as he didn't know where Brent had his cabin, and nobody saw him go out after he and his wife retired for the night,' I say. I look about and it seems nobody wants to volunteer more.

Nick Matthews, a fit man in his early thirties, says, 'I wouldn't rule Mitch out. Friend or not, he had a violent argument with Brent, and I think the fact that Sally was sexually assaulted may have played on his mind. As well as that, being drunk might have loosened his inhibitions.'

'Possibly,' I say.

After another review of the evidence board I'd prepared showing each of the friends as well as Herb Petrov, with photos and brief profiles underneath, I turn to the team. 'We're back at square one. We need to start over. I'll assign each one of you to go through the stories and data again. Unless something jumps out at us, Amanda and I will talk to each person again. Also, I might get you all to increase the background checks of each of the friends to see if something else emerges. Okay, if there's nothing else…,' I say.

Amanda raises her hand. 'Brent, it seems, was not well liked by anyone, apart from Mitch. Is it possible that he'd told people when he'd be at the Hydro and one of his enemies planned to kill him, knowing that each of the five friends would be suspected?'

'I agree Amanda. Good point. Who's been through his social websites? Perhaps he'd made his comings and goings known.'

"I checked his Facebook account,' says Rita, a big woman with a poor sense in fashion. 'Nothing specific was mentioned, only a comment that he was having a four-day long weekend in the mountains.'

'Good Rita, well done. Would you go back to that site and check out his Facebook friends to see whether we need to interview any of them?'

'Okay, will do,' says Rita.

I ask Amanda to come back to my office as the others are heading out of the conference room. Then I say, 'What do you think, if need be, that we re-interview the five suspects to see if something pops?'

'Sounds reasonable, if we have no other leads,' she says. Amanda is wearing tight trousers today and it's distracting.

'Would a follow up by other members of the team produce better results?' I offer this suggestion just to consider other methods.

'I don't think so. We're familiar with the body language of the suspects and should be able to detect subtle changes if our questions hit the mark,' she says.

'Great, that's what I was thinking but I needed confirmation from another perspective,' I say.

Amanda stands and before leaving, says, 'I've broken up with my ex-boyfriend again. I was foolish to imagine things could improve.'

'Oh,' I say, not really knowing what to say. This statement will only stir up emotional turmoil and I don't have time for that right now. I add, 'Now you'll be able to focus all your energies on the case.'

Amanda steps outside to let me deal with how I feel about her as a single woman again. It's going to be tough for me to ignore her and I wonder whether she's playing with my mind.

TWENTY

Friday starts out dismally. Clouds roll in and rain pours in Collaroy. And probably also in all surrounding suburbs. Sydney has such a vast area that I don't know whether rain was dampening the entire city and adjoining towns or not. But I didn't go for a morning jog. I could have made the effort and I have done it previously in this kind of weather but today, I'm not in the mood. After breakfast I drive to Bondi Road and wait outside the Panel Beaters where Ken Morton works. I have nothing specific in mind. I just want to get a feel of the people and activity at 8 a.m. At around 8:10, Ken Morton drives in and parks his car, a second-hand Mazda, at the side of the yard. He struts into the workplace entrance. After a few more minutes, I leave.

I drive my car to the train station at Bondi Junction and catch a train to Parramatta. Walking to Headquarters, I buy two cartons of coffee. I drop one off on Amanda's desk.

'Thank you,' she says, acting surprised.

'My pleasure,' I say, striding off to my office. I got wet on my walk here, but the rain had eased sufficiently for it not to be a problem. Besides, I was able to get here undercover for most of the walk.

At noon, Rita pokes her head in the door. 'Are you free?'

'Yes, please come in and take a chair.'

Rita is wearing slacks and a dark shirt and flat black shoes. 'I was able to check Brent's friends on Facebook and there are three guys who went to high school with him. Here's a list with telephone numbers and addresses, both personal and business. One had moved interstate, so he won't be any use, I suspect, but you can make that call.'

'Is Grant Michaels included?'

'No,' says Rita, 'that's odd, isn't it?'

'I guess. Then maybe Grant had moved on as he said to us and didn't agree to be friends on Facebook. Perhaps Brent wouldn't have included ex-high school buddies on social media unless he actually liked them.'

'Right,' says Rita, looking puzzled. 'Should I examine Grant Michaels' Facebook?' She straightens the strands of lank hair which have fallen across her face.

'Why not. It can't hurt. And while you're at it look at all social media accounts used by the five friends,' I say.

Rita gets up and leaves me with the handwritten information on my desk. I thank her for a job well done. It may prove instructive or it may not, but we need to cover all bases. I make some calls and collect my jacket on the way out of the office.

I get Amanda to join me on the way out of the building, take a squad car which I'd booked and drive to Castle Hill.

'What gives, boss?' Amanda says in a cheeky voice.

'Watch it. You may need to be disciplined if you carry on in that tone,' I say, smirking.

'I'll take that risk,' she says.

This is a perfect opportunity to continue flirting and to assess whether she'll be up for something over the weekend, but I think better of it. 'Rita came up with two names which may prove useful. Three actually, but only two in Sydney. It turns out Brent had high school pals with whom he kept in touch. Yet, from university, he only continued an association with the five that we already know of.

Funny right? I don't keep in touch with anyone from high school and only two guys from university.'

'But then you're not a people person, are you?'

'Maybe not. I gather you are,' I say, driving more quickly than the speed limit. I've made an appointment with Gary Prentice before embarking on this journey. I use the navigation system to find the street I'm after.

'I still have a few girlfriends from the past and some current ones,' she says.

'So, you're a party girl?'

'Not at all. But I'm no hermit either.'

"Nor am I. I'm discerning, that's all.'

Getting closer to our destination, Amanda asks where we're headed.

'A decorating business. This Prentice bloke is a manager there,' I say.

Gary Prentice is a man who looks like he played rugby league or rugby union. Solid with cauliflower ears. He ushers us into a back room after we introduce ourselves.

'What's this about? I've had a clean record for five years,' Prentice says.

'We're not here to talk about you,' I say, although I was aware of his minor charge of assault outside a pub years ago.

'Ok,' he says, folding his arms across his chest.

'Did you know a Brent Morton in high school?' I ask.

'Sure. I still see him,' he says.

'I doubt you will, to be honest. He's dead.'

'Dead!' Prentice gasps. 'How? When?'

'He was murdered recently We're here to know more about him to try to establish who may have had a grudge against him,' I say.

'It might be a long list,' says Prentice. 'Brent and I played football together, but that was years ago. I know he pissed people off, even in high school.'

'Give me an example,' I say.

'He would play practical jokes on both guys and broads.'

'That's pretty normal in high school, I would think.'

'Yeah, but he went too far sometimes. I can't remember the details, but I know some guys threatened to tell teachers, but they never did. Brent was big for his age and he had a reputation of fighting and beating kids up. With girls he would touch them on their butts or pussies, excuse the language, Miss. But it happened.'

'Don't worry about it,' says Amanda, 'I've heard plenty of blokey words in this job.'

Prentice laughs, 'I bet.'

'Did anyone take serious offence?' I ask.

'Probably some did. But what could they do?'

'That was a long time ago,' I say, 'It would be a bit far-fetched to think they'd get even now.'

'You're right. Who would? I can't remember most of the people I went to school with, let alone what we did or talked about.'

'Okay, thanks for your help,' I say, and I turn to Amanda. "Do you have any questions?'

'Do you recall a Grant Michaels?'

Prentice laughs uproariously. 'Oh yeah, the poof.'

'He's homosexual?' I ask.

'I don't know. But Brent would make fun of his ways. Grant was bright, always came top of the class, but he didn't do traditional guy things. He liked chess, didn't hang out with any group. He had friends, but they were one-on-one friends, if you get my meaning. He was a nerd. So, Brent called him a homo. And after a while the name stuck, and everybody called him that.'

'I see, that's instructive.'

Once we're back in the vehicle, I turn to Amanda. 'I could kiss you. That's the breakthrough we've been after. You are clever and well…'

'You can keep going. I love the flattery,' Amanda says.

'Don't want your head to explode,' I say, stepping on the accelerator.

'Aren't you going to ask me out either?'

I look at her. 'I'm game if you are. Thought you may have had enough of men, given your recent turmoil and split.'

'That's over. Let a new chapter begin.'

TWENTY-ONE

I PULL THE SHEET ASIDE and slide out of bed. After a few stretches, I open the curtains.

It's a warm Saturday morning and I feel jubilant. The day is gorgeous, sunshine and blue sky and if I didn't know better, birds are singing all around. But, of course, there are no birds around. It's in my imagination.

My positive view of life is based on three factors. I now believe Grant Michaels is the killer. I know of one of the men responsible for killing my parents all those years ago. And finally, and perhaps the most important is that I'm meeting Amanda tonight.

I complete a short run then wade into the surf and swim for twenty minutes. Refreshed, I head home, shower, dress and walk to a café for breakfast. I grab a newspaper to see what's gone on in the world. Usually, I find reading the news depressing. Often there are disasters, mayhem, murders, political stupidity, and celebrity nonsense reported. But today I'm oblivious to the troubles appearing in print. I eat my food, drink my coffee, and focus on the entertainment section. Tonight, I'm taking Amanda to a show, the theatre, something I rarely have time for.

Amanda insists on meeting me in the city as she says it's madness for me to drive from Collaroy to Strathfield on the other side of town and then back into the city. We meet outside the Capitol Theatre thirty minutes before the start.

'Hope you like musicals,' I say, after giving Amanda a hug.

'I've wanted to see Jersey Boys for ages. So, great choice,' says Amanda.

We have a glass of champagne before going in. The show proves to be surprisingly uplifting and my mood hasn't dampened all day. This is unusual for me as I'm prone to find fault with people or something else. I wonder whether Amanda is good for me or it's simply a fluke, a one off. I'll see, I guess.

After the show, I take Amanda across to Chinatown and we find a place to eat. We allow the waiter to choose, as we're both unfamiliar with good Chinese cuisine. I've been to Hong Kong and experienced fine dishes, but I can't say the same for my choices in Sydney. Amanda told me she enjoys Thai and Japanese but hasn't had many Chinese meals. So, we'll judge the choices the Chinese guy makes after tasting the four dishes he'll bring to us, which we'll share.

'Do you really think Grant Michaels killed Brent?' asks Amanda as we sip our white wine.

'I do. I thought he was altogether too smooth.'

'That doesn't make him guilty.'

'Agreed, but we have something to focus on now, rather than flying around in circles. At least we'll attempt to find evidence which confirms what I believe.'

'And if we find nothing to connect him?'

'Then I'll reconsider. Besides, we have other team members tasked with other approaches. I'll take two team members off the general search and have them assist us,' I say, as the first two dishes arrive. The other two dishes arrive soon after.

We eat and converse about the food, having had enough shop talk. Finished, I pay the bill, telling Amanda to put her money away. Outside the restaurant, I wave a taxi down.

'You didn't drive?' Amanda asks.

'No. I wanted to enjoy a few drinks so since you came in by train, I thought I'd take a taxi in.' I open the door for Amanda as the taxi comes to a halt. I slide in next to her in the back seat. I give the driver my address.

'We're going to your place?' Amanda asks, surprised. 'We haven't discussed this.'

'Do you want to go somewhere else?'

'I don't know. I'm not used to having someone decide for me. You're not my boss tonight,' she says.

'No. I'm not your boss and you can bail anytime. Just tell me,' I say, giving her every opportunity to opt out. In my experience, I've found most women, not all women, prefer to have decisions taken out of their hands. At times, I've been agreeable for them to decide but few can make up their minds.

Amanda remains silent and the taxi drives over the Harbour Bridge. We both look out the window. I admire the city lights and atmosphere of a large metropolis. I can't see what Amanda is looking at or whether she's reflecting on private thoughts. The worst thing that can happen now is for one of us to ask the other what they're thinking.

Inside my house, Amanda walks around observing the simplicity of my abode. It has a functional kitchen with a metallic fridge, a breakfast island and cooking facilities. The living room has a large flat screen television, a sofa and two armchairs. No clutter. My study has a bookcase, a desktop computer and storage for files and paperwork. The bedroom has built-in wardrobes, a king-size bed, and a bedside table on which sits a light stand and a digital clock radio. The second bedroom has a single bed and a cabinet which houses my trophies from sport. The bathroom is clean with a shower stall, a medicine cabinet, and a toilet.

After Amanda has gone through the entire house, except for the balcony overlooking the ocean, she says, 'Wow. How neat it is. I didn't think bachelors lived like this. How many teams of cleaners did you employ?'

'Ten,' I say, slapping her on the butt. 'You imagine that all men are messy, I gather.'

She turns to me and we kiss. The rest of the night is sheer pleasure.

* * *

Amanda lies in bed, having woken to the sound of sirens in the distance. She looks over and finds Hank fast asleep. The time emitting from the digital clock shows its 4:12 a.m. She finds the darkened room, the soft rhythm of faraway waves soothing. She reflects on the night out with her boss. She loves the fact he was organised with tickets and how he planned the dining and take-charge approach to go to his place, not relying on the back and forth many men would resort to. But she'll have to be careful, she doesn't want to abrogate control. But the whole evening worked like a charm. Of course, this was effectively a first date. Future dates might be hard to compare to this one, if this night were a benchmark she wants to set. But she is realistic. Fairy tales don't exist.

Amanda turns on her side facing the man who made her climax more than once. She listens to Hank's light snoring purr. A bit like the family cat she had growing up. She closes her eyes. But sleep proves elusive. She thinks about Hank's take on the murder. Why is he so certain Grant is the perpetrator? She found Grant to be a charming man, polite and well presented. She could imagine him being gay or considered as such, but appearances are deceiving, she feels. But she has to confess, she was delighted when Hank thought she'd been instrumental in making the breakthrough.

Later in the morning, Amanda wakes to sunshine streaming through the window. She figures she must have fallen asleep as she ponders what to say to her companion who is now smiling at her. He hands her a cup of coffee. 'Up sleepy head, it's getting late and you're wasting the day.'

'What time is it?'

'Nine o'clock. I've been awake for an hour and I've even been out for a run.'

'God. How slack of me,' she says, but not meaning it. Can't he chill out, she wonders? It's Sunday.

TWENTY-TWO

IN THE OFFICE ON MONDAY morning, I ask Rita to pop in.

'Morning boss, what can I do for you?'

'Sit down,' I say, 'how was your weekend?'

'Okay, I guess. Nothing out of the ordinary. A family Sunday lunch,' says Rita. She's almost shocked, I can see from her expression, that I ask about something personal. She doesn't associate me with friendly chats. I can't believe it either. Either I'm losing my touch or being with Amanda Saturday night has softened me.

"I'd like you to turn up everything you can on Grant Michaels. Social media, reviews from his university days and later employment and anything else you can think of.'

'Okay,' says Rita, without commenting further. A split second later, with no further instructions, she gets up and leaves.

Around eleven, I walk past Amanda's desk and ask whether she'd join me outside for a coffee. 'Get all your chores done yesterday?' I ask.

'Sure. Even did grocery shopping for a week. What did you do with your free afternoon?'

'Nothing much. Watched some cricket and a Netflix movie,' I say.

'When do you get your chores done?'

'Haven't I told you? I was left a healthy inheritance. I've invested wisely, and I can afford cleaners and others to do my chores.'

'Lucky you.'

'Sort of. But I miss my folks and I'd rather have them alive than the money they had,' I say.

'What happened to them?'

'It's a long story. Here we are. Your turn to buy the coffees, isn't it? I'll have a large Cappuccino.'

Walking back in the sunshine, clouds all but disappeared, Amanda asks, 'Do we interview Grant Michaels again?'

'Not yet. Once we've got more information, we'll ask him to pop into Headquarters,' I say.

'You're experienced in these matters. How's your old cop partner taking it?'

'Fine. He's a pro. This switch in partners for one case doesn't bother him.'

'Boss,' begins Amanda.

'Yes, my sweet,' I say.

'You'd better be careful. Actually, we'd better be careful. Do you think anyone suspects that we're close?' Amanda asks, as she avoids bumping into a pedestrian.

'I've already had my boss tell me about potential sexual assault and that I could lose my job, if there's so much as a whiff of impropriety.'

'Aren't you worried?'

'I should be but I'm not.'

'What if you mistreat me and I report it?'

I look at Amanda to see if she's serious. 'I cannot predict the future. All I know is that I'm unable to help myself as far as you're concerned so I'll take that risk.'

'That's sweet of you to say. OF course, I would never do the wrong thing by you. I may be stubborn at times or even difficult to get along with, but I've never been vindictive.'

We continue back to the offices without further discussion.

As I examine my emails, I see nothing new on the case. I sit back and reflect on what Amanda had said about not being vindictive. But when love is involved, and it turns to hate, those kinds of actions emerge. Many crimes are committed in the heat of the moment, ones not previously contemplated. However, I wonder whether Grant Michaels had planned Brent's murder down to every detail.

I get up and walk into the homicide squad area. I see Joe standing talking to Nick. I summon Joe into my office.

Joe is a rangy looking man, around twenty-eight, with the crew-cut of his fair hair almost making him seem bald. He's not a bad looking fellow except for his crooked teeth. Only evident when he laughs or yawns. When he's seated, I ask what's he up to. He mentions his work plans, then I tell him, I have a new assignment: to tail Grant Michaels and tell me what his movements are for the next week, including the weekend.

'When do I sleep?'

'Take somebody with you and you can rotate the surveillance.'

Just when Joe's gone, Amanda comes in. 'May I talk to you?'

'Of course, what is it?'

Amanda sits down. 'My mother is very ill, having suffered a stroke, and my father is overseas on business. I need to be with her for a few days.'

'Naturally. Take all the time you need,' I say.

'She's in a Brisbane hospital so I can't even check in from time to time,' she says.

'Don't worry. You attend to her and don't worry about the case, okay?'

'Thanks. I feel silly and I'm truly sorry.'

'Why. These things happen. Part of life. Go,' I say. I want to kiss her but it's far too risky. Instead I drink in her essence, the way she looks and smells and how I remember she feels.

At five o'clock, I receive a call from Candice Berry. 'I need to talk to you,' she says mysteriously.

'Okay, what's on your mind?'

'Not over the phone. I live in Lane Cove. I'll text you the address. Come over tonight.'

I'm intrigued. What could be so important that it needs a face to face. I'm surprised she hasn't suggested a public place. But now I'm being silly. I guess I'll go with the flow and follow up, as Candice has suggested.

TWENTY-THREE

THE STREET HAS CARS PARKED on both sides making it awkward to find any space for my vehicle. Eventually I do find a spot, but I need to use all my skills to back my car in without touching other cars. I'd gone home first, had a shower and a bite to eat before embarking on my journey to see Candice. I'd also studied Google maps to find the address she'd texted me.

I get out of the car only to note that it's darker than one would expect in a suburban street because a couple of the streetlights aren't working. Walking along the footpath, a woman with her dog, a Labrador, walks towards me. She says hello as she passes. The dog stops to inspect something, and I pause, turn and pat the bushy haired white creature.

'What's his or her name?'

'Ruby,' she says.

'Lovely dog,' I say, moving on. I've always loved dogs and I thought, if I ever settle down, I'd get a large dog, a German Shepherd or a Rottweiler. If we had a dog like that growing up, perhaps my folks wouldn't have suffered the way they did. But I can't dwell on Ken Morton now, that's for another time.

After finding the flat number given to me, I knock on the door which opens almost immediately.

Candice is dressed to kill. Low cut blouse and a micro skirt. Perhaps I was wrong all the time. Candice killed Brent, making him weak at the knees with an outfit like this, then plunging a knife into his neck as he bent down. 'Come in,' she commands.

I obey, squeezing past her, unable to avoid my body brushing against her boobs. 'Hi, you wanted to talk?'

'Yes,' please take a seat. 'Would you like something to drink?'

I think about this. I'm on duty but maybe not so much. But I do need a drink, as this feels like an ambush, albeit a pleasant one.

'Scotch on the rocks, if you have it?'

'Scotch coming up. Hope a Ballantine's is acceptable.'

'Certainly.' After a quick glance at the well-decorated living room, I sit on a sofa.

A moment later, on the beige sofa, I'm nursing a glass of scotch whiskey with ice cubes while Candice, sitting opposite in a leather armchair cradles a glass of white wine.

'Okay,' I say after taking a sip of my drink, 'You wanted to tell me something.'

'Yes. Something occurred to me today when I met one of my friends for lunch. She and I spoke about people from uni, and then I remembered seeing somebody at the Hydro Majestic the weekend we were there. Thought I'd better tell you because this guy and Brent were not friends. And I had no idea whether he was there for a break or to track Brent.'

'Name?' I ask.

'Matt Dunbar.'

'Did he see you?'

'Yeah, he waved to me but carried on with his mates. They were going outside,' Candice says, her micro-skirt riding up as she crosses her legs exposing her knickers.

'Why did this guy and Brent have differences?' I drink more scotch, enjoying the sensation as it slides down my throat, burning on the way down.

'Not sure but I recall Matt insulting Brent then pushing him when Brent stood his ground, laughing at Matt and calling him an arsehole. This happened when Brent and I came across him at a pub years ago.'

'And Brent didn't push back?'

'Brent was much bigger than Matt and the push was feeble.'

I take out my iPhone and record Matt's name in the Notes app. This is one feature I use more than most. Beats having to carry around a note book.

'While we're talking about this topic Candy, were there many people who disliked or hated Brent?'

Candice gets up, places her glass on the coffee table next to her and sits on the edge of the sofa, next to me, her boobs inches from my nose. 'There were some, but then you probably had guys who didn't like you and wanted to beat you up too,' she says.

I know I should move away or simply get up and go but I'm a guest and I don't want to be rude. 'In primary school I was bullied but as I grew older and taller, I got into boxing and later cage fighting.'

'So, you can take care of yourself,' Candice says, putting her arm around my shoulders, her boobs now pressing against my face.

'Not always,' I say, as I realise, with consternation, I'm helpless now. I might suffocate at any moment, but I'll accept the punishment in good spirits.

Candice slides onto my lap and she kisses me. Her lips are so soft and her whole body is luscious. Why couldn't this have happened if I didn't have Amanda in my life?

The long kiss ends. To have a chance to think, I ask for another drink. Candice fills up my glass which gives me time to tell her I have another appointment in half an hour.

We have our drinks and I stand, thanking her for the information.

'Next time you're nearby, drop in,' Candice says as she opens the door for me.

Wandering half-dazed back to the car, I wonder when I was so lucky to have two magnificent women keen to be with me. I can't recall another instance. That night I sleep soundly.

* * *

Amanda arrives in the hospital to find that her mother is in a ward after an operation. Her mother is sleeping, and Amanda takes a seat by her side. A nurse pops in and checks the patient's vitals, ignoring the woman lying in the bed next to her. The nurse pulls the curtain around Amanda and her mother.

'How is she?' asks Amanda.

'As well as can be expected,' she replies then walks out of the room.

Amanda looks at her phone. She's contacted her father who said he was flying home from his business trip. No further message from him so she imagines he's on the flight from Jakarta. There's no message from Hank either and she wonders what he's doing.

Amanda waits for an hour then goes down to the cafeteria, on ground level, for a cup of tea. She uses the time to consider how to gain evidence against Grant Michaels. She's not convinced he's guilty but acknowledges that Hank has had more experience and that he may be right in his theory.

When she returns to her mother's ward, she finds her mother is awake and pleased to see her. Amanda gives her a peck on the cheek and asks whether she wants anything.

TWENTY-FOUR

THE SUN FINALLY APPEARS AFTER a morning of dull grey clouds hanging overhead. I had thought it was going to rain and dampen the mood for golf. I stand in the Pro shop and examine the equipment for sale. But I decide not to buy golf bags and clubs and balls as everything is too expensive for the occasional game. I hire the relevant set of clubs and a buggy and go outside.

John, a retired police officer, finally turns up. 'Sorry mate, traffic,' he says.

After we're both ready to play, we head for the first hole. John tees off and hits his ball at the first attempt straight down the fairway. Now it's my turn. I place the small round ball on a tee and take a few practice swings. My first serious swing goes over the ball. John smiles but keeps his remarks to himself. I try again, this time connecting. The ball flies off to the right into a thicket of trees, as though the white projectile has a mind of its own. I curse silently. We move on.

The game takes about two hours to reach the ninth hole. Once we complete this hole, John suggests a beer. We visit the clubhouse, buy schooners and sit outside on the balcony admiring the view over the green course and beyond, out to the ocean. The Mona Vale course is conveniently located close to my place and not much further from John's place.

'What's new at the squad?' John asks. John retired from Homicide two years ago and keeps in touch by inviting me for a game of golf, a passion of his, every few months. I go along although golf is not my game.

'Not much. A few murders, some new personnel but we're still doing stuff you're familiar with,' I say, not wanting to talk shop.

'Ron Pritchard hasn't transferred to your unit, I suppose,' says John.

'No. He's still in the city.'

'Last time I spoke to him and I mentioned your name, he said he came across an old file relating to your parents' case.'

'Really? That case was never solved,' I say. My heart beating faster, I lean forward. 'Why did he tell you this?'

'Well, it appears a DNA test was done on material held in evidence. It seems one of the killers had left a mark on your father's belt. Must have been used by the perp to pull your father along the floor with it. In 1990, DNA was not available. But the guy wasn't on the system, so it still doesn't help.'

'I see. Too bad.'

Our conversation continues but revolves around politics and sport. We agree to forego playing the next nine holes and have another beer. Then we head off, shaking hands and saying we need to get together more often.

That night, around nine o'clock, I call Amanda. 'Hi there Mandy, how are you holding up?'

'Let me get out of the room,' she says, and I wait a few minutes before she speaks again. 'Mum's recovering but she seems weak and when she's released, she'll need looking after.'

'You expect to be there for some time?' I ask.

"I can't say. But as soon as I know, I'll call you,' says Amanda.

'Okay. I didn't realise you're from Brisbane,' I say.

'I'm not. My father retired recently although he still has a job as a company director and they moved up here, the Gold Coast actually, to be in a warmer climate.'

'If he's a company director, he must have money,' I say.

'What do you mean by that?'

'Nothing really. Can't he hire a carer once your mother's well enough to go home?'

There's a momentary pause then Amanda says, 'He's a director of a private company and he doesn't earn much so no, we're not rich. Certainly, we can't afford the care you're talking about which is very expensive.'

'Sorry,' I say, realising I've put my foot in it. Because I say what I think sometimes, I'm destined to offend. 'Let me know how it's going, won't you?'

'Of course. Any progress on the case?"

'I'm waiting on the report from the Michaels' surveillance team to see where that leads. I need to be patient so it could be another week or two. In a way, it's a good time for you to have a break.'

'I wasn't after a break,' Amanda says, her voice signifying annoyance. 'And looking after a sick person is not having a break.'

'What I'm getting at is that there's not much you can do here on Brent's murder. I have other members of the team working on different angles, just in case I'm wrong about Grant.'

'I see. I'm sorry. I'm tired as I haven't slept much and I'm worried about mum,' says Amanda.

'I understand. Anyway, I'll talk to you again in a few days.' I don't see the value in talking to Amanda every day.

* * *

I call in sick which is unusual for me. I've never done it before. But then I've never been ill. I sustained some minor injuries when I engaged in UFC fighting during my twenties and early thirties, but they were never serious enough for me to take time off. Besides, I was usually the one dishing out punishment. I still miss UFC contests, but I realised a long time ago that, sooner or later, in contact sports, more serious injuries would eventuate. I wasn't keen to have that happen, so I retired while I was ahead. Twenty-one fights, twenty wins, one draw.

However, I'm not sick today. I'm going to take the day to watch Ken Morton and to collect his DNA. Then I can match it with what has been stored. And if there's undeniable proof that Ken Morton is guilty of my parents' deaths, I'll act. I'm not sure how yet. After all, I'm not allowed to investigate this crime because of a conflict of interest. This won't stop me searching for the truth. And if the man is guilty, I'll need to consider how best to seek justice.

Dressed in gear which would make a homeless person balk, I loiter around the Panel Beater's in Bondi Road. I've covered my head with a hoodie and a blackened face, using smudges of dust and dirt to disguise my features. I know it's going to be a long, boring day but I'm mentally prepared. I can't take a book but, if I find an old newspaper, I can use that to read and further cover myself, if required.

At around eleven o'clock, Ken Morton comes out of the shop with another man. They light up cigarettes and find a spot away from the entrance and puff away. The two men seem to be friends as they share a joke as they enjoy their break. After they finish their cigarettes, both drop the butts on the ground and grind them down with their boots. They go back inside.

I shuffle into the yard and I get a strange look from another man who emerges from the Panel Beater's.

'Hey, what are you doing? Get out of here, this is private property,' the bulky shaven-headed man says.

I stoop and pick up the cigarette butts which Ken Morton and his mate have dropped. I have no idea which is which. 'Smoke, mate.'

The man comes closer. 'Just scat you bum.'

I shuffle back outside. Having achieved my objective, once I'm out of sight, I walk to my car, parked some blocks away and drive off at a fast clip. I feel lucky. I have Ken Morton's cigarette butt earlier than I'd thought possible. I was prepared to watch him for several days, if necessary, even taking leave time, if that's what it took.

Now, the next challenge is to match the DNA from these samples to the sample kept in storage.

* * *

Amanda talks to the doctor who has just examined her mother. She has followed him out into the corridor and asked him to spare a moment. The doctor, a man who looks impatient and harassed, nods as Amanda speaks and asks about her mother's condition.

'I'll know more this afternoon. You need to be patient,' he says then strides down the hallway as though he has a train to catch.

Amanda is annoyed. She doesn't want to be here, but she has little choice. Her father has been at the hospital the night before but has gone again. She realises she's the only person who'll be able to look after her ailing mother. As an only child, she can't even share the responsibility.

She wants to call Hank but won't. He's busy and what can she say to contribute to his day? As the doctor pointed out, she'll have to be patient. She returns to sit with her mother. She picks up a women's magazine and she'll read articles to her mother to cheer her up.

Amanda knows she could suggest her mother go into a home, but she won't contemplate such a move. Her mother has always been good to her and she believes it's her responsibility to return the favour.

Amanda begins reading an article on the Royal family, something her mother finds fascinating.

TWENTY-FIVE

Ron Pritchard is a tall slim man who stoops a little as he walks along. I've been able to meet with him at his office in the city Friday morning. I explain what I've done and pass the cigarette butts over the desk to him in a clear plastic bag I had in my car. I had arranged for John to alert him so that my call wouldn't come out of the blue.

'You don't really believe this is going to help, do you?' Pritchard enters his office and sits behind a desk, cluttered with papers, a couple of empty coffee cups and a photo frame. I sit in a visitor's chair opposite him.

'I don't know,' I say, 'But I need to try.'

'I'll arrange the test, but I wouldn't raise your hopes. The DNA we found is not your father's or your mother's because they've been eliminated but it might be somebody not connected with the murder,' he says.

'I understand. But I would appreciate you doing what you can,' I say.

'Okay, but you'll owe me a beer,' Pritchard says.

'No problem,' I say, getting up and shaking his hand. 'John tells me you're interested in joining the Homicide Squad.'

'I was at one point but I'm reconsidering. My wife isn't well, and I might retire to spend some time with her. She has cancer, you see.'

'I'm sorry to hear that, Ron.'

'I'll be in touch,' Pritchard says, lowering his rangy frame into his chair.

The weekend comes and goes without incident. I'd called Amanda on Sunday and told her I wish she were back in Sydney. She said she'd like to be but can't. I enquired about her mother and she updated me, but the news was not positive.

Back in the office, Monday, I work on administration. I'm waiting for the DNA results which Pritchard knows are sensitive, given they're being done as a favour to me rather than as part of an official investigation. He's said he would place a rush on the order and keep it secure. Finally, at 3:20 p.m. Monday, I get a call from him.

'Results are in. We were lucky that one of the men had a drink driving charge and had DNA tests done previously. But it wasn't only Ken Morton who happened also to be on our database. So, we can't be certain that Morton is implicated. The second DNA on the belt matched with the other man's cigarette stub, a fellow called Doug Jones.'

'Thanks Ron. I owe you. Next time I'm in the city, I'll call you.'

'Sweet. Take care.'

'Will the case be reopened, and this man investigated?' I ask before finishing the call.

'It's not my case but I'll talk to the chief.'

'Thanks,' I say, not expecting anything will happen, knowing the politics which go on.

I hang up. I have a lot to ponder.

Is Jones the other man involved in the ancient murder? It makes sense. Morton and Jones are buddies. They robbed my parents, and something went wrong so they killed them. I don't know why they did what they did and they're not likely to admit anything even if brought in for questioning. It's all too hard for the department, I imagine, so I doubt justice will be served. Only I can deliver justice. And, as a dedicated police officer, can I even contemplate that? A dilemma only I can resolve. Nobody else would be able to understand what I've gone through over the years. The pain I suffered when I was young seeing my parents massacred was raw and it took many years to recover.

I lean back, satisfied that I know what I know but unable to formulate a solution. But I need to get back to the case on hand, ironically, to find Ken Morton's son's killer.

That night, as I'm about to pick up a novel to read, Amanda calls.

'Hello, nice to hear from you. How's your mother?'

'She's not well. We're at home in Broadbeach and she's going to need looking after. I've resigned from Penrith police. Had to go through the right channels and I'm sorry to leave you in the middle of a case but I'd rather you hear it from me than through departmental communication,' she says.

'Oh,' I say, totally taken aback. I don't care about her not being on the case, but I've got feelings for her. Seems I'll always lose out in the relationship stakes. 'That's bad news. What about your home here?'

'I'll deal with it, but I thought you should know,' she says, her voice breaking up. She concludes the work news then asks how I am.

'I'm fine but I miss you.'

'I miss you too. Lousy timing.'

'Will you return to Sydney one day?'

'I don't know. Everything is up in the air at the moment. Look, I need to go. Take care,' she says sniffling.

I throw the novel against the wall. I'm feeling miserable. I want to have a large scotch, but I have none at home. But I need something to soothe the disappointment.

When I knock on Candice's door, it's almost eleven o'clock.

'Hi,' she says.

'Hope it's not too late, although I'd...'

Candice grabs my hand and pulls me in. 'Come in.'

'I was wondering if you still had some scotch,' I say.

'Of course. Take a seat, I'll get you one. I've had a bugger of a day at work and I could use a stiff drink myself.'

We drink our poisons and soon, looking at each other, it's inevitable that we cosy up and kiss. Then she pulls me into the bedroom, and she strips. No matter how much I would drink, nothing could prevent me getting hard after seeing her naked. I walk over to her and we allow a moment to take every facet of our existence into account. It's great to be alive, I reflect, all other concerns dissipating like smoke up a chimney.

We make love, slowly and yet, urgently. My brain is on autopilot as my body celebrates the skin to skin contact. Candice seems to move in such a way as to complement my actions. I close my eyes for a moment to allow the sensuous feeling to envelope me. Then I open them again to take in the wonderful visual. The experience is mind blowing as I can't imagine a drug taker having a bigger high.

Exhausted after two hours, we lie side by side, holding hands. There is no speech. It's totally unnecessary. We both drift off to sleep.

* * *

I sneak out of Candice's place at 5:45 a.m. with my pants and shoes on but carrying my shirt. I find my car despite being somewhat dazed. I'm probably still over the alcohol limit to drive but I hope it's early enough so as not to encounter much traffic. On my drive to Collaroy, I think about the night, how it came about and my rash decision to see Candice. I now know that stress makes me want sex, not alcohol or drugs.

I should feel guilty, but I don't. It wasn't my decision for Amanda to stay in Queensland. I choke up when I think of Amanda and imagine what could have been. But it's pointless thinking like that. I'm not normally sentimental but, I have to admit, with Amanda, I come close. I get to my house without incident. No police cruisers, no accidents, no roadblocks.

Rather than going to bed, I get ready for work and arrive so early, I have time to eat breakfast out, other than at my desk. When I get back to the office, I feel invigorated.

After carrying out some research into Matt Dunbar, I find he has a criminal record for assault. Convicted and served one year inside. Currently he lives in Dundas which is not far from here. He works locally too in the building industry. Before heading out, I get a second cup of coffee from the kitchen.

'Hi Hank,' says Jill, 'Not like you to make your own coffee.'

'I'm quite capable,' I say turning to see Jill who has her cup in hand, ready to get her tea. She is older than me by three or four years but appears older than her years because she dresses like a mature woman rather than one who is keen to stay fashionable. Long dresses, flat shoes, stockings and glasses are her usual garb.

'I was going to talk to you later, but since you're here you might as well know that one of your team, Amanda Walsh, has resigned for personal reasons,' says Jill, dropping a teabag into her cup.

'Okay, thanks,' I say, taking my coffee back to the office. No wonder Amanda called me. I'd hate to have to deal with the news of her resignation like this. It was enough of a shock, coming from Amanda, but to have Human Resources tell me in such an off-hand way would have been worse.

I make some calls and find where Matt Dunbar is working. I have another member of the team come with me. We arrive at a building site in Parramatta and ask for Dunbar. We're directed to a man who is wearing a blue singlet tucked into long grey trousers. I introduce myself and my colleague.

'Can we talk somewhere private?' I ask.

Dunbar is a man with a paunch, but he still looks muscular. He wipes dirt from his right arm and stares at me. 'What's this all about? I haven't done anything,' he says.

'Would you prefer to talk at the station?'

'No. Follow me,' he says leading us to a hut.

'We understand you were at the Hydro Majestic a few weekends ago,' I say.

'That's not a crime, is it?'

'Not yet,' I say. 'You know Candice Berry, is that right?'

'I know her but not well,' says Dunbar.

'What about Brent Morton?'

'Oh yeah, that cunt. I used to play football against him. He's a real arsehole.'

'Why do you say that?'

'He's not a sporting person like others in the team. When his team lost against us, the other guys would shake hands and accept defeat graciously. Not Morton. Instead he throws insults. He's just a jerk. Why?'

'Did you see him at the Hydro that weekend you were there?'

'No,' says Dunbar, looking puzzled.

'Can somebody vouch for you?'

'Yeah. I went up there with some mates, all of whom can vouch for me.'

'Okay Mr Dunbar, here's my card. Email me those names please,' I say.

'What's this about?'

'This is a murder investigation. Brent Morton was murdered at the Hydro Majestic.'

'Wow. Thank the guy who did it,' he says, laughing.

I walk off and I can't help smiling. The Morton family, from my perspective, have their share of enemies. And Dunbar expressed his view clearly.

Driving home, thinking of Amanda, I get a call. I have Bluetooth, so I can respond without touching my phone.

'Yes,' I say.

'Hi there, it's Candy. How was your day?'

'I got things done. But I'm tired. Didn't get much sleep last night,' I say. I'm not sure whether I'm pleased to hear from Candice or not. I shouldn't really be involved with her until the case is over.

'You and me both. But I had a lovely day thinking about you and what we did last night. What are you doing tonight?'

'I'm meeting a mate at the pub,' I say.

'Too bad. What about later in the week?'

'Sounds good. Let me check my calendar later.' I need to assess what's possible, and also if Amanda has definitely made up her mind about staying at the Gold Coast.

A UFC mate calls me before I leave for the pub to say he can't make it. In a sense, that suits me as I'm keen to have a quiet night at home.

TWENTY-SIX

Joe sits in front of me. He's a dark-haired man with a muscular upper body and an earring through his left ear. His hair is cut short. 'I've prepared a report, but I wanted to give you a brief summary,' he says.

I swivel around to face him squarely. 'That's great Joe. What have you got?'

Joe coughs, takes a drink of water then says, 'We've followed Grant Michaels for a week. Friday night, after work, he had drinks with colleagues in a city pub. Details are in the report,' he says.

'That's fine, I can look at them later. Just need an overview now,' I say. Joe knows that I like the bottom line on things rather than fuss with details when they're not relevant.

'Saturday night, he and his girl go to a posh restaurant in Double Bay. Most nights he stays in. Then, on Monday, we follow him to a gay bar near Taylor Square.'

'Excellent work. Send me your report today. Also, since I've lost Amanda, would you be my partner for the rest of this case?'

'Sure boss. What do you want me to do?'

'I'm going to read a couple of statements again then I want you to set up separate meetings with Fiona and Grant.'

'At Headquarters or at their home?'

'No, not yet. We'll talk to them at their offices,' I say, not wanting them to be at home together when the interviews take place.

Joe leaves and I find the appropriate Word documents easily.

We meet with Fiona at noon. She's taken a lunch break and I introduce Joe before we sit at a round table in a conference room at her company's premises. We all fill our glass with water from a jug containing the cold liquid.

'Nice to see you again, Fiona,' I say, 'Sorry to take up more of your time but there are some things I don't quite understand.'

Fiona smiles, it's a false smile, a professional one intended to disarm us. 'I'm all ears.'

'Okay. I've reread both your and Grant's statements from Medlow Bath and I can't figure one thing,' I say, looking directly at Fiona. Today she wears a shade of red lipstick and nails, I notice, but a shade I'd be unable to put a name to.

Fiona keeps her eyes on me but says nothing. Her attire of black slacks and a white tie-neck blouse attests to the fact that she is professional and used to being cool under pressure.

'You said you headed back to your cabin around 1:15 a.m. yet Grant says he returned at 1:30 a.m. Why is there a gap in the times you stated? Didn't you go back together?'

'I can't explain that. I don't think either of us were looking at our phones so late and therefore the time didn't register. Grant has a watch, but I only use my phone to check the time.'

'Did you return together?'

'I thought so but I'm not completely sure.'

'How can that be?'

Fiona scratches her forehead, the first sign of her losing her composure. 'My memory is of us leaving Brent's cabin together. But I had quite a lot to drink so I can't now visualize getting to our cabin. That's all, a memory lapse.'

'Okay. Thanks Fiona,' I say. 'Should your memory come back to you in the next few days, please call me.'

Joe and I sip some water then stand and shake Fiona's hand.

* * *

Grant Michaels agrees to see us in his office today. It's 3:15 p.m. and he says he has fifteen minutes before his next meeting. I don't say anything to upset him. I could have used the line about coming to a police station but all I want is for him to feel comfortable. I believe he is clever and if I scare him into thinking he's a suspect, he'll lawyer up immediately.

'Thanks for seeing us Mr Michaels. Just wanted to check something we found when analysing your statement.'

'I understand. You need to cross the 't's and dot the 'i's, like we all do if we want to do a good job,' he says, hands clasped in front of him, resting on the small meeting-room table.

I sense that's he nervous although he puts on a front of extreme confidence. He even has his jacket on, probably something he does with his clients. 'You said you and Fiona went back to your cabin after one o'clock. Did you both go back together?'

His eyes roll upwards as though he's pretending to think. 'I think we did. Can't recall exactly. Why? Is it an issue?'

'Not really but as you say we'd like our records to be accurate. Still, you mentioned returning at 1:30 a.m. Did you look at your watch?'

'Yes. I was thinking about the next day and our plan was to drive to the Jenolan Caves, and I was trying to calculate how much sleep we'd get.'

Joe asks, 'Do you need lots of sleep?'

'Not particularly,' Michaels says, glaring at Joe as though he were an irritant he'd like to crush under his shoe.

'Fiona's recollection was that you returned at 1:15 a.m. Why the discrepancy?' I ask.

Michaels leans back. 'I don't know. You'd have to ask her.'

'We did,' I say.

Michaels looks at his watch. 'I have a meeting to get to. Is there anything else?'

I stand as does Joe. Joe says, 'Nice watch.'

'Thanks. A gift,' says Michaels.

'Anyway,' I say, 'I appreciate one can't be precise about the time. Thanks for seeing us.'

We shake hands and leave.

Outside, I say. 'He remembers alright but he's playing games with us.'

'I think you're right. Cagey character,' says Joe.

Before getting back in the squad car, I call Fiona's mobile phone. I wait for a moment and wonder whether she knows my number and is refusing to answer. Eventually she picks up.

'Hello,' she says, sounding a little annoyed.

'Hi Fiona, sorry to be bothering you but could you tell me when you were at the Hydro, what were the plans for the weekend? I mean, were the six of you going to trip around or stay put?'

'We had no plans to leave the hotel during the period we were there. Maybe some walking, that's all. Why would you need to know?'

'I don't know,' I say, 'Just wanted to get some context. Anyway, thanks.'

In the car which Joe is driving, I say, 'Michaels was lying. 'He never planned to visit the Jenolan Caves. We'll apply more pressure as soon as we carry out another week's surveillance.'

'Okay boss. It's not going to be an exhilarating experience.'

'Yeah, I know. Afterwards, I'll buy you a beer,' I say.

'That's terrific. What I come to work for,' says Joe, smiling.

'Great. I knew you'd love it.'

Back at the office, I open my emails and find that I have two administrative ones, three relating to past cases and one from Candice. I click on the one which is private. Candice says:

Dear Hank,

> *I know you are a busy man, and I shouldn't be doing this at work. But I can't help myself, I'm into you and I think I like you too much, maybe even love you. From the first time I saw you in the mountains when you questioned me, I felt something.*
>
> *This is unusual for me. I've had past relationships that had become serious, but you've affected me like no other. I*

want to tell you this because otherwise I'll hate myself if I don't get to say what I mean. Life is too short to be with the wrong person or alone.

Come over on the weekend. I want to see you so badly but if you don't want me or you can't because you have another woman in your life, I can deal with that. But I want you to say it to my face. Please don't ignore me, I can't live with that.

Yours,
Candy

I sit back, not quite believing what I've just read. Is she genuine or pulling my chain? I've never received a love letter or anything close to it before.

On my way home, I think about the two women who seem to be in my life. Amanda, sweet, sensible, intelligent and compassionate. But she's not available. Then there's Candice who's chasing me. This is novel and, in a way, pleasant. She's brash, sexy, wild. I get home and change into casual clothes. Without having thought things through, I get into my car and drive to Candice's.

I walk up to the door and hear voices inside. I stop, not knowing whether I'd be welcome. She may have another lover there. If that's the case, I need to know. If she has others, then all that posturing about loving me is just that, posturing. Then I won't have to feel guilty when I ignore her. I knock, two hard thumps.

When Candice answers, she looks surprised. 'Hello, come in,' she says.

I enter and sitting in a chair is a young woman dressed in bright colours.

'This is Amy,' says Candice. 'Amy, this is Hank.'
I nod hello.
'I've got to get home, so I'll leave you two alone,' says Amy who gives Candice a peck on the cheek. She says goodbye to me and vanishes out the door.

'Hope I didn't interrupt something,' I say.

'No, no, not at all. Amy is a friend who had a problem she wanted to talk about. But she needs to get home to her family.'

'Right,' I say, 'I got your email.' I take a seat on the sofa I'd sat on the night Candice came on to me.

'Would you like a drink?' Candice is standing, looking at me with her large almond-shaped, green coloured eyes.

'No thanks. I just came over to understand what you meant.'

'Really. Wasn't I clear?'

I shift around in my seat, feeling a little foolish. I don't want to admit I couldn't comprehend what she'd written. 'I guess it's unusual to fall in love so quickly. I want to be sure you actually mean that. We've only been to bed once.' Having finished saying my piece, I feel silly. Am I interrogating a suspect for loving me?

'I don't have to go to bed with someone to either like them or love them,' says Candice, coming closer.

Today Candice is dressed in more conservative clothes, black trousers and a white blouse and shoes with low heels. Still, she looks marvellous. As she comes closer, breasts straining against her frilly top, my heart beats faster. I say, 'You're right, of course. Never happened to me like that, is all.'

'You poor man,' she says, sitting on my lap. 'Maybe there's only one person for you and only one for me.'

Having her top-heavy body push into my face ends the discussion. I wasn't going to argue. Now I'm trapped unless I want to carry her off me which I don't. She pulls back, takes my face in her hands, and kisses me on the lips. I return the kiss and we are crushed together for a long time. Finally, she unlocks her lips and gets off me.

'I'm hungry,' I say, 'have you eaten?'

'Not yet. I could make something that's in the fridge.'

'Don't go to any trouble. I'll shout you to a pizza. There's a great place not far from here.'

'Let me freshen up first,' she says.

Twenty minutes later, Candice and I are sitting in a family-oriented pizza restaurant but it's too late for families and only young couples grace the inside seating. The menu is basic, but I've eaten here before and the food is great. I even recommended this place to a colleague.

Candice has changed into a short skirt and a T-shirt which advertises her bra-stretching abilities. I'm mesmerised and need to look into her eyes to stay focused on what we're here for: to eat.

'How's the case going?'

'I can't really talk about it. But we did check out the bloke you mentioned,' I say, reaching her hand and holding it.

Candice forgets about the case, saying, 'Do you feel about me how I feel about you?'

I stop myself laughing. I'm definitely lusting for her, but I don't know whether that's love. My feeling for Amanda was more loving but she's not around anymore. I need to forget her, put that potential monogamous relationship behind me and live my life as best I can. 'I'd like to find out.'

Pizzas arrive. We eat in relative silence, enjoying the food as we're both hungry after a day at work. Candice offers to pay half, but I refuse and pay the bill with my credit card. Then I accompany her, on foot, back to the unit she owns. Outside I kiss her but decline coming inside. I know what would happen.

'Thanks for coming over and the meal,' Candice says.

'It was my pleasure.'

'When will I see you again?'

'Let's see how our calendars are this weekend.'

Driving home, I have mixed feelings. Candice is sexy and available, and she wants me. That's not bad: it's extremely positive as this doesn't happen much. Then there's Amanda. I don't know how long she's going to be in Queensland. But does she like me the way Candice does? I can't imagine a long-distance relationship working. It's not for me. I need to be able to see somebody regularly.

TWENTY-SEVEN

THE SAND ON AMANDA'S BARE feet feels warm despite the time being nearly eight o'clock on a balmy Saturday night. She is at Broadbeach, minutes away from her parents' house. She hears the waves as they lap the beach.

Amanda sits down and watches the ocean and the lights of Surfers Paradise in the distance. This is a magical time at a magical place. She is wearing shorts and a tank top. She lies down and looks at the stars. If only she were here with Hank. She wonders what he's doing right now.

It's been a few weeks since she's come to the Gold Coast. Her mother is not getting better but tonight her father is in the house. He wants to put her mother into a nursing home where she can be looked after properly. They argued and discussed it for a few days and Amanda is sick of the subject. She said she's happy to be with her, and be the carer, as they cannot afford a full-time care person. And to be put into a nursing home, they'd have to sell the house.

Amanda closes her eyes. What they've finally decided is that they will reverse mortgage the house, place the mother into a nearby facility and both the father and daughter will work. Amanda will transfer to a police station near Broadbeach. That's the plan. Amanda is reviewing the plan in her mind, again. She thinks she might call Hank to get his perspective on this idea. She found he had unusual ways to sort out problems.

Amanda is about to get up and walk along the beach when she feels sand hit her face. She brushes it off and opens her eyes. Two teenage youths are standing over her, gawking.

'Looking for some action, honey?' says the shorter sandy-haired youth.

'Go away and leave me alone,' says Amanda.

One of the youths jumps on top of her and tries to kiss her lips. Amanda moves her head and rolls over on top of him. The other youth lands on her back. She screams and the youth on her back gets up. A couple who are strolling along the beach see the commotion and the man calls out, 'What's going on?'

The youths run off. Amanda gets up and brushes the sand off herself. With her training, Amanda believes she may have fought the two young men off but two against one would have been difficult. She's glad the situation resolved itself peacefully.

The couple come over. 'Are you alright?' asks the woman.

'Yes, thanks for being around. I may have had some problems if you hadn't walked by,' says Amanda.

'Would you like us to call the police?' the man asks.

'No thanks. I'll do it myself. Thank you and enjoy your walk.' Amanda watches while the couple, hand in hand, continue on their way. Amanda walks back to the house. She is glad she hadn't brought a wallet with money, cards and other important documents to the beach as she may have been robbed too. She checks that her phone is still in the pocket of her shorts. But she doesn't call the police.

* * *

Another week has gone by and I'm without female company. Amanda is stuck in Queensland and Candice has been asked to go to Perth by her company to carry out training. It's Sunday morning and I'm considering my strategies for the next week. But my mind keeps going back to Mandy and Candy. Funny how those names are the same except for the first letter. Now another thought drifts through my mind. A threesome with Candy and Mandy. I shake my head before it explodes.

I eat breakfast out, at a nearby café where I'm a regular, as I'm feeling too lazy to make anything. I think about calling Mandy and Candy but I won't. It'll be too distracting and there's nothing I can do with them so far away. I've always been a visual guy, not so keen on phone talk.

My Eggs Benedict arrives. I've already had one coffee but before the waitress goes, I order another Cappuccino. It's a warm day with a refreshing breeze and I want to use it profitably.

The Brent Morton murder hasn't produced a break-through although I'm still convinced Grant Michaels is our number one suspect. What if Candice killed Brent? She had motive and, if she had carried out the crime, I've compromised the investigation by sleeping with her. And if she is such a good actress, should I get close to uncovering her as a killer, then my life would be in danger too. But I dismiss the thought as quickly as it formed. I simply can't imagine that I'm such a bad judge of character.

Another surveillance report on Grant Michaels is due tomorrow. For me, the more pressing matter is getting the killers of my parents punished. What I have managed to achieve over the last week is information about Doug Jones, the man whose DNA was on my father's belt.

Doug Jones is fifty-one years old, twenty-three when he and Ken Morton carried out the home invasion on my home. The home invasion which left me an orphan. The brutal home invasion which ended with my parents' deaths. The home invasion which has never been solved. And why did these men kill? For nothing more than to steal some jewellery and cash kept in my father's safe.

Jones lives in Bellevue Hill now in a block of units on Birriga Road. I discovered over the past week that he had been in trouble a lot as a young man. He'd been arrested for theft but escaped conviction for lack of evidence. He'd been convicted of aggravated assault. He was in prison for merely twelve months for that infraction. I've always thought the penal system in Australia was too lenient. Once Jones came out of prison at the age of twenty-eight, he began doing boxing as a sport.

At home, I dress professionally, with dark trousers, open-necked collared shirt and polished black shoes. I take my warrant card, badge and hand cuffs and make a call. On the way over to Jones' unit, I consider my approach.

I park my car up the hill on Benelong Crescent, a street directly opposite the block of units I'm visiting. My phone call proved that Jones is home. I hung up when he answered. He may have thought the call was a wrong number or a charity worker who didn't like his gruff tone. It doesn't matter what he thought, I think. I couldn't care less.

The time is ten minutes to eleven when I knock on the door of a unit one level below ground. I wait a moment and the man who answers is the same man I've been watching for a number of days and nights. He wears shorts and a loose T-shirt. Barefoot. Scruffy light hair. Unshaven.

'Mr Jones?' I ask.

'Yeah, what about it?'

I flash him my warrant card and as I guessed he didn't ask to see it closely. But he's seen warrant cards before and knows I'm a cop of some kind. 'I'd like to ask you a couple of questions,' I say.

'Bugger off. I haven't done anything. Where's your partner?'

'He's waiting upstairs,' I say. 'May I come in?'

He walks inside, leaving the door open, allowing me to follow. I close the door and walk in. 'I understand you know a Khalid Mohammad,' I say as I walk into a rectangular living room from which two other rooms are visible.

'Yeah, so what?' Jones sits on a sofa which has seen better days. He also lights up a cigarette.

'I need to ask you about him,' I say, remaining standing.

'No way. I know my rights.'

'I'll need to take you into the station for questioning then.'

'What for. You can't come in here like some jumped-up cowboy.'

'Khalid Mohammad has been arrested on terrorism charges and we are interviewing his associates,' I say.

At that moment, I sense somebody behind me. I turn to see a thin blonde woman with a pan in her hand. She swings but I step away and avoid contact. Then I use my UFC skills and kick her in the stomach. She falls but I feel a punch on the side of my head. I wobble but don't fall down. Before Jones can deliver another hit, I raise my arm and fend off his fist. Then I kick him in the groin, and he doubles up, groaning.

Without waiting for any response, I knee Jones in the head. He falls down. Keeping an eye on the woman who had crashed into the wall, I wrench the arms of Jones behind his back and cuff him. Leaving him on the ground, I collect the frying pan and threaten the woman with being beaten and tell her to go back into the kitchen which is located on the other side of the living room wall. She obeys without another word. I tell her to find the car keys for a vehicle I know Jones owns. She brings them to me, looking frightened.

I bundle Jones into the boot of his car, a battered Toyota Corolla. He protests but I punch him in the ribs and tell him to shut his mouth. I drive for nearly an hour to an abandoned house I'm familiar with. It's in the delightful suburb of Cabramatta, a place with a large population of Vietnamese. The house is one which has been home to drug dealers who have been pushed into government accommodation: prison.

I drive into a garage, grab Jones from the boot and take him into a room which I'd set up earlier. I force him to sit in a sturdy wooden chair and bind his arms and legs with heavy industrial strength rope. He struggles as I work on him, but I subdue him with a headlock and partial choking. Then I use a Hypodermic Needle, collected from a felon, to render him helpless by jabbing him in the neck. The needle contains Etorphine, a substance which works instantly. I learned about this from the television show 'Dexter'. I undo the handcuffs and pocket them. I leave the premises.

Jones is still tightly bound to a chair when I return. He's somewhat groggy but beginning to wake up. I took the opportunity while he was unconscious to find a place which sells coffee. Picking up a bottle filled with water I pour some over him and offer him some to drink. He takes a mouthful and spits it out at me. I grab his right ear and twist it until he screams.

'Settle down,' I say, 'Any more drama and you'll invite real punishment.' I sit on a chair facing him.

'Who are you? What do you want?' Jones sneers at me.

'I'll ask the questions. Just sit back and relax. If you behave, I'll let you have some water to drink. Understood?'

Jones nods.

'Tell me about Ken Morton,' I say.

'He works with me.'

'I know. But he's more than that, isn't he?'

'Okay, so he's a mate. We go out drinking sometimes.'

'Who was the woman at your place?'

'A girlfriend. She's only been with me for a month or so. Why?'

'Does she live with you?' I lean back.

'No. It was a sleep over. Can you loosen the rope, it's burning into my wrists.'

'What's her name?'

'Maureen White. I usually go to her place. Why?'

Knowing she doesn't live with Jones is positive for me. She's less likely to care about him, particularly if she heard he might be implicated in terrorism. Also, she's less likely to call the police although I can't rule that out completely. Still, she has no real evidence against me. What can she say? A cop picked up her boyfriend to question him. It wouldn't score high on their plausibility register. 'How often do you see your ex-wife?'

'How do you know about her?'

'I know a lot about you. So, let's get down to business.'

'What the fuck are you talking about?'

'You and Morton carried out a home invasion twenty-eight years ago, right?'

Jones' face alters to show surprise. A brief flash of recognition registers in his eyes. 'I don't know what you're talking about.'

'That's what I thought you'd say. However, we have DNA evidence which places you at the scene. What do you say about that?' I stare at him, watching his eyes carefully.

'That's not possible,' he stammers.

'You pulled Mr Rockwell by the belt, closer to the safe, didn't you?'

'I can't rem…' Jones stops talking.

'Go on.'

'I want a lawyer,' he says.

'So, you were there?'

'I'm not saying another word,' Jones says, obstinately.

'I'll leave you here to think about it,' I say.

'You can't do this. I know my rights. This isn't a police station, is it?'

I don't respond. Instead, I walk out and drive the battered Corolla back to Birriga Road where I park the car to the exact spot I'd found it. I wipe my prints off all areas I may have touched, collect my vehicle and go somewhere to have lunch.

At six o'clock I return to where I'd bound Jones. I see that he has soiled his shorts. He looks distressed.

'Want some water?' I ask.

He nods. I figure he's too parched to talk. I get him to open his mouth and then I pour water in. He drinks greedily, this time not spitting it out. I wait until he seems able to talk.

'You're torturing me. That's not allowed,' he says.

'Who says?'

'Jesus, you're a sadist. What's in it for you?'

'Tell me if Ken Morton was your partner then I'll tell you what's in it for me,' I say.

'Yes. Ken and I did it. It was so long ago. Who cares?'

I look at Jones with sheer hatred. I want to let him die of hunger and thirst, but I can't if I want to remain true to the badge. I could kill him and Morton, and I know where to bury the bodies without them ever being found. A pig farm where the animals will devour every part of the flesh and bones. 'I'm Hank Rockwell. I was in the house when you raided it. You're lucky I'm a real cop so you will live.'

'Fuck, all those years ago. We only wanted the jewels.'

'Then why did you kill the hostages?'

'That was Ken's idea. He said they'd squeal because the old bastard was so stubborn, he'd only tell us the combination when we threatened to cut his wife.'

'Thank you. I bring out my phone and stop the recording.' I give Jones a picnic bar, shoving it into his mouth. Then I inject him again to render him helpless. I untie him, making sure when he slumps forward that he doesn't hit his head on the hard floor. With some effort, I lift him and carry him over my shoulder to a bed in a bedroom at the house. I tie him to the bed. Then I call Ron Pritchard, my city contact, and advise him of everything he needs to know to collect Jones and arrest Morton.

Ron Pritchard tells me he'll take care of it and won't inform anyone of how the information was obtained. The confession will be enough to add to the DNA evidence as well as the ruby worn by Grace Morton which will be confiscated and matched to items stolen in the robbery.

TWENTY-EIGHT

EXHILARATED BY MY DAY'S WORK, I want to celebrate. I ring Candice and agree to collect her from her home at eight o'clock. I think of Amanda but, as she isn't around, I can't do much about it. Wouldn't it be wonderful, I fantasize again, to be in a threesome with Amanda and Candice? But as I get to Candice's flat, I once more dismiss this crazy idea.

'You're looking cheerful,' says Candice as she opens the door.

'Ready?' I ask.

'Yes.'

'Great, let's go. I have a reservation at a wonderful restaurant in Crows Nest.'

We're sitting at a table with a white cloth spread across it, a lit candle in the centre and a bottle of French Champagne open to my right. Candice and I clink our flutes and sip the refreshing bubbly.

'Here's to you,' I say, 'and to a successful day.'

'Did you find Brent's killer?'

'No. Another case was resolved though.'

'Do you always celebrate closing a case in this way?'

I look at Candice who hasn't disappointed me in looking sexy and glamorous. I smile. I'm happy. Getting the men who killed my parents is a significant victory for me but I'm not going to reveal this to anyone. It needs to remain my secret. 'Of course not, but things turned out well after this case, twenty-eight years old, has finally been put to bed.'

'Here's to you, my love,' says Candice.

The waiter comes to the table, as silent as a ghost, before faking a slight cough, to take our orders. Candice screws up her face as though it's all too hard, then finally settles on Calamari for entrée and Atlantic Salmon for the main course. I'm less conflicted and ask for King Prawns as my entrée and Wagyu Fillet Steak for my main outing. As well as that I get the waiter to select a wine which would suit our choices.

Halfway through our meal, Candice says, 'This place has a great atmosphere, and the food is exquisite. Do you like French restaurants best?'

'Not necessarily but the service here is second to none and I do like the food.'

'Good choice. I'm glad you brought me. This would be a place Grant would love.'

'Does he enjoy French meals or posh places?'

Candice finishes a mouthful of fish then says, 'Mr Perfect. He'd like the whole thing. Great service, fine wines, excellent food offerings and faultless taste.'

'Is he a connoisseur or enjoys everything to be of the highest order?'

'Both, I guess.'

'What do you think of him?' I ask, keen to get another person's view of the man.

'Not my type. He'd bore me to tears. He has no passion. But he does like everything in its place. Fiona who dresses like a model suits him to the ground.'

'He seems to dress well and he's so neat, I thought, at first, he was gay.'

'He comes across like that, but I don't think he is.'

Sated, we end the meal with coffee.

'How's your partner, you know, the brunette with the nice skin?'

'You mean Amanda. She's gone to the Gold Coast, personal reasons.'

'Oh. I thought you two had some chemistry,' Candice says, eyeing me with interest.

I can't believe how perceptive she is. 'I've worked with a number of partners, but Amanda was my first female partner.'

Candice fiddles with her coffee cup. 'How did you find that?'

Aware that females are jealous of others when they're in a relationship, I formulate my response with care, 'She was professional. I had no reason to be critical.'

Candice doesn't ask any more about it, but I suspect she doesn't believe me. When I take her back home, she says she's tired, so I kiss her goodnight and watch her disappear into her block of flats.

* * *

Amanda sits on the living room couch, drinking a cup of tea, reflecting on her day so far. She'd got up early. She'd checked in on her mother who was asleep but breathing erratically then went to the kitchen to fix her some breakfast. When she popped into her mother's room again, her father who has been sleeping in the spare room to get decent sleep, was there, looking at his wife with a frown.

'She's looking grey, don't you think,' he says.

'My God, what's happened?'

'Wish I knew.'

'We better call an ambulance.'

Now, pondering the situation, Amanda feels drained from the emotional toil. Her father has gone to the hospital with his wife. He told Amanda to stay put, to get some rest. But Amanda is not able to go to sleep. The worry is keeping her frozen. She realises she needs to overcome this inertia. Work would be the solution.

TWENTY-NINE

THUNDER AND FLASHES OF LIGHTENING wake me. Rain is streaming down. It's only six o'clock in the morning. The thunder reminds me of Amanda and the night we spent at the Hydro Majestic. I get up, peek outside, and realise that I won't be going outside for a run or anything else.

I open my computer to see the news. Flash-flooding, rescues of people trapped in cars, Parramatta dam overflowing and causing flooding. Chaos on the roads too. After showering and dressing for the day, I read more articles, then check the news on television.

At 8 a.m. I make the decision not to go to Headquarters. I call in to say I'm working from home. I have access to work files, and I'll spend the day indoors mostly. I'll pop out when the weather provides a break for some food and coffee but otherwise, I'll do catch up duties on paperwork and other cases.

At ten-thirty, I take a break. Before going out, I call Amanda. 'Hello, Amanda, is that you?'

'Sorry, I've just come from the hospital where my mother has just died,' she says.

'Jesus, I'm sorry for your loss. You poor thing,' I say.

'Thanks. How are you anyway?'

'Good. Sydney's had torrential rain from early this morning and I'm working from home.'

'How's the Brent Morton case coming along?' Amanda sniffles.

'We haven't cracked it but I'm still working on it,' I say, looking out the window and noting the rain still falling but less forcefully than previously.

'I have to help dad arrange for mum's funeral but I'm considering coming back to Sydney. Do you think I'd be able to get my old job back?'

'Of course. If the Brent Morton case is still going, you'd be able to continue here. Joe is my current partner but you're prettier.'

'Flatterer. You haven't changed.'

'I don't know. I can't judge whether I've changed or not. Look, if you are returning, let me know and I'll see what I can do to have you reinstated.' I end the call. If Amanda were to come back, I'd have a dilemma on my hands. But then she did lead me to believe she'd be away permanently. Why should I feel guilty about seeing Candice?'

I get to my car, parked under the block and use the remote to open the car door, then drive to Warringah Mall in the rain and I park on the east side building's second level which is undercover. I won't get wet doing this. Taking the escalator down, I walk on the first level of the Mall and come to a small café called Jamaica Blue. I order a Cappuccino and a pastry. I call Joe.

'Have you done a follow up report on the surveillance of Grant Michaels?'

'Yes, but I haven't put it on file yet. I'll email it to you if you want?'

'That'll be good. I'm at home today so I'll catch you tomorrow.'

'Okay. It's taken me twice as long to get to work. Damn weather.'

'Miserable if you're commuting. See you Joe,' I say just as my snack and coffee arrives. Rather than using the time to think about the Brent Morton murder case, I think about Amanda and Candice and what might happen if either one gets wind of the other. But as people settle into seats around me, I dismiss my potential dilemma.

Back at home, I open my email and see that the report from Joe has arrived. I open the attachment which reveals the details of Grant's movements over the last few weeks. I read the day to day movements, then the summary prepared by Joe. He's a man, I conclude, who likes routine. Each Friday he networks with investment bank colleagues. Most nights he stays indoors with Fiona, except that Fiona did venture out two nights without Grant. Saturday nights are date nights, it seems. Perhaps Grant has read about having time set aside to ensure the relationship continued successfully. Then there was one night when Grant again visited a gay bar.

I sit back to understand this. He didn't visit such a venue on a regular basis, only twice during the entire time he was being watched. It doesn't mean he is gay. But it is curious and something I want to explore. However, I wonder whether a man is the best person to question him about this. If Amanda were to return soon, she might be the right person to present such an enquiry.

While I'm contemplating the best way to get Michaels to tell us the full story of that night at the Hydro, I listen to Andrea Bocelli and Sarah Brightman's "Time To Say Goodbye" on Youtube. Music often stimulates my creative thinking.

* * *

At six o'clock that evening, I get a call. A homicide. Details are released, and I change from my casual gear to more suitable clothes to brave the wild weather. In the streaming rain, I drive towards the city on Pittwater Road. As I get closer to Dee Why the wind buffets the car and I wonder whether I should stop and wait out the torrents of water on the road. Cars coming towards me are travelling slowly because there is no possibility that safety can be preserved should they pump the accelerator in peak hour with branches flying and visibility reduced drastically.

Luckily, I know the Northern Beaches area well, so I turn left into a street which takes me to a street parallel to the ocean front road. After parking I walk down the road to the building where the incident took place. It's easy to spot as there are flashing lights of police and ambulance vehicles. When I arrive, walking under the police tape, I show my warrant card to the uniforms posted to keep civilians away. Not sure why they bother as the rain and wind make it unattractive for people to be outside in this weather, unless they have to be.

When I scale the stairs to the second level flat, I find Joe Torino already there, standing in the hallway. Apparently Forensic and other personnel are inside.

'Thanks for the report on your surveillance of Grant Michaels,' I say, looking about. 'What's happened?'

'Woman stabbed in the kitchen and her daughter is hysterical. Haven't spoken to her. She's in a bedroom, crying.'

'Let's see what's going on,' I respond, walking down the hall and, off the left-hand side of the flat, I observe the various people examining the floor and walls. The body of a woman of around sixty, I guess, is lying on the tiles, blood evident on the floor surrounding her. Deep gashes appear on her upper torso.

'Seventeen stab wounds, detective,' says a man wearing Forensic gear.

I peer at the dead woman. Mixed ethnicity. Dark hair, slightly overweight. 'Witnesses?' I ask.

'The daughter but she's incoherent right now,' the Forensics guy says. He points towards the back. 'In her room.'

I look at Joe. 'Do we know who did this?'

'The daughter called it in, but we have no further information,' he says.

'Okay, let's talk to her.' I walk to the back where the bedrooms are located, with Joe following. Joe has Italian looks, dark and brooding, because he is Italian. However, his parents came to Australia when he was seven so there is no hint of any accent except Australian.

I knock on the closed door. Two of the three doors leading to the bedrooms along the long corridor are open showing the rooms to be empty, so the daughter is obviously in neither. 'Hello, please open the door. This is detective DS Hank Rockwell.'

'Go away,' somebody says.

'I'm sorry, that's not possible. If we need to break it down, we will. One last chance.'

We wait a moment longer. Then the door cracks open and a pale face belonging to a young woman stares at me. The face is blotchy with tear stains. The thin female, seemingly a teenager, uses her sleeve to wipe away more tears.

'May we come in?'

The door opens wider and the teenage girl turns back to her bed and sits down. Joe and I walk inside and stand opposite her. The room has pop star posters on the yellow walls. The bed is unmade, and clothes are strewn over a chair and all over the floor.

I get the impression she's not going to speak unless prodded, so I ask, 'What's your name?'

'Beryl.'

Beryl is five foot three, I figure, with dark curly hair, tattoos on her bare arms and a ring through her nose. I can never understand why the young despoil their skin and appearance with ink and metal. But then I may seem old and outmoded to them. 'Hi Beryl. I'm Hank and this is Joe.' I want to be as informal as possible because I think getting anything from her might be difficult. This is where Amanda would have been useful.

She nods.

'Can you tell us what happened?'

Beryl tucks her legs under her bottom. 'I heard an argument coming from the kitchen,' she begins then stops.

'Was it your mother and father?' Joe asks, taking notes.

'Our father left years ago. My brother, Kevin, was shouting and my mother was saying mean things.'

'Okay,' I say, 'go on.'

'Then I heard piercing screams, loud shrill screams. I put my hand over my ears.'

'What then?' asks Joe.

'I heard the front door slam shut. I went out and saw mum on the ground, blood everywhere.'

'Then you called the police?'

Beryl nods. 'But I had to see whether mum was alive. And she wasn't.'

'What was the argument about?'

'I don't know. But I heard mum call Kevin stupid. As stupid as Donald Trump.'

'And Kevin ran off. On foot?' I ask.

'Yes.'

I turn to Joe. 'If it hasn't been done yet, get a search party out to find him.'

Joe leaves the room and I walk over and check that Beryl is okay. 'I'll get somebody to come and look after you.'

Later, when I'm driving home through the rain, I realise that the young man was made to feel something he resented deeply. It occurs to me that Grant Michaels may have the same kind of hang-up, about something. Was it his early life at home or at school?

THIRTY

KEVIN BATTERSBY IS SEATED AT the station's interview room. Joe and I observe him through the two-way mirror. This is the first time Joe's been my partner. I found out more about him when we were enjoying coffee in a quiet part of the building. He grew up in Concord, a suburb boasting many families of Italian ancestry. His father was a restaurant owner and his mother stayed home to raise three sons and one daughter. Joe is the oldest son at twenty-eight and was keen to join the force after spending hours watching police dramas on television.

We discuss our strategy for interviewing Kevin Battersby who was picked up last night not far from his house by a patrol car which had been alerted to watch out for a man running. He was thoroughly drenched. Having left the young man in the room for forty minutes, we walk in and Joe sets up recording and visual equipment. I introduce Joe and myself, and ask for Kevin to state his full name, date of birth and address.

After the preliminaries are over, I tell him his rights and ask whether he wants to be represented by a lawyer. Battersby is a pimply youth who seems like a shy kid. He has tears welling up and shakes his head. I gather this to mean he doesn't want legal representation, at least not at this stage. Perhaps, like others in the interview process, he'll change his mind once he doesn't like the questions.

'Tell us what happened last night, in your home,' I say looking at Battersby's eyes.

'I didn't mean it. It was an accident,' Battersby says.

'Seventeen stabs into your mother's torso is an accident?'

'No, no. But she said so many mean things I just lost it. I didn't mean it.'

'So, you concede that you stabbed her?'

Battersby weeps uncontrollably. I wait a moment and terminate the interview.

On the way back to my office, I wonder whether bringing Grant Michaels in would have the same effect. Somehow, I doubt it. But it was good to have solved one murder so quickly. A far cry from the Morton and Jones caper.

Just before five o'clock, I walk into my superior's office. He's reading a magazine and ignores me until I'm standing before his desk. His PA has gone somewhere so he's not been warned.

'Yes, what is it?'

I fill him in on the Kevin Battersby situation and he grins. 'Well done.'

'Why don't we arrest Grant Michaels and put some pressure on him?'

'The investment banker bloke?'

'That's right.'

'I don't think so. We don't have enough, if anything, except a theory to go on. And he'd sue the department if we got it wrong.'

Just as I thought – gutless. He really doesn't care, except for his image and that of the department. 'Alright, we'll keep at it,' I say turning.

'Good. Goodnight,' he says to my back.

* * *

Amanda is excited. Looking out of the plane, she sees the Sydney skyline. Home, she thinks. Although she's given up her Strathfield place, she was able to rent a flat in Bondi, on a temporary basis. Once settled in her temporary abode, she will find something more suitable, she believes. But it would be great to live in the Eastern Suburbs.

She sits back, closes her eyes as the plane descends, and thinks about her life to date. She was born at the Royal North Shore hospital and the family lived in Cammeray. They moved to Burwood when her father got a job south of Sydney and his then commute from Cammeray was gruelling. When she moved out of the family home, she found a flat in Strathfield, close to her parents' home. Then her father semi-retired and he and her mother moved to the Gold Coast. But Amanda had a job by then and she loved Sydney, so she stayed.

She thinks of Hank and wonders whether it is too late to continue life with him. Of course, she realises that she can't just barge back into his life and she needs to tread carefully. But she understands, now that she's been interstate and was intentionally distanced from him, that he means more to her than previous boyfriends did.

A bump onto the tarmac jolts her back to the present. 'Oh,' she cries, opening her eyes.

The woman on her left says, 'That was a bit rough. Qantas are usually better at landing these things.'

Amanda smiles. She's alive. It doesn't matter.

She takes a taxi to a hotel on Campbell Parade in Bondi. Tomorrow, she'll claim the keys for the flat she's rented. Tonight, she will settle in, have a quiet meal, walk along the promenade and get to bed early. She's been reassigned to the Bondi Beach Police station and will start on Monday. Tomorrow, Sunday, she'll sort out her new place. New furniture and other domestic items need to be purchased. It should be fun, she thinks.

She considers calling Hank but decides that's not a good idea yet. She may be needed on the Brent Morton case, but she doubts it. It's been too long since she contributed, and it may remain open for some time. The five weeks she's been away have flown by so quickly and a lot in the case must have changed.

Amanda registers at the hotel desk and takes her luggage upstairs by herself. There she drops the cases and lays on the bed. It feels so good to be back in Sydney.

* * *

I'm nursing a large cup of coffee in a favourite café of mine on the foreshore of Dee Why where cafes stretch along the street, side by side. I feel relaxed and happy. Across from me sits Candice, her red hair swept up in a bun, revealing a lovely pale neck. It's a warm Summer's day and breakfast is being served. I wait a moment while the waitress places plates of food before us. I have bacon, eggs, tomato and sourdough toast. Candice has French Toast with strawberries, maple syrup and ice-cream.

'How was the flight?' I ask.

'Too long. But knowing I was going to meet with you this morning made it tolerable,' says Candice as she strokes my hand.

'Why did you have to stay there on Saturday?'

'Some problem with the audit. I had to sort out some queries otherwise it would mean I'd have to go back next week. Which I didn't want to do. I'm just tired of the travel.'

'Why don't you quit?'

'I might. It's been on my mind for some time, actually.'

I'm not sure whether she's genuine but it doesn't matter. 'Job changes are usually a big decision.'

'What about you? Do you want to be a cop for the rest of your life?'

'Unless I get a better offer,' I say glibly. I enjoy catching the bad guys and I'm not interested in making money at a job which doesn't excite me. I hope Candice is not the type of woman who wants to change me. If so, the relationship is doomed.

After breakfast, we walk along the promenade which leads to a pool and beyond that rocks which people like to scale. I've lived on the Northern Beaches for most of my life and I've always liked the ambience. From Palm Beach to Manly, the water invites surf-board riders, body surfers and swimmers. Balmoral Beach does not generate large waves so is more suitable for families with young children and those folks keen to simply wade. I take Candice's hand and lead her across Dee Why's rocky terrain. We stand, and watch waves crash into the sides, water splashing before us. It's a marvellous sight.

'Brent was keen on the water. He liked surfing and he was a strong swimmer. But he was also keen on diving,' says Candice.

'What about the rest of your group?'

'The friends who met annually?'

'Yes.'

'We all liked to enjoy the water, swimming, and body surfing except for Grant. He was more of a sailor, liked sitting in boats or more specifically on yachts.'

'Not keen to be in the water?'

'Not really,' Candice says, dragging me back to a kiosk to get more ice-cream.

I follow and wait while she gets two cones and hands me one. It's vanilla which I like. I notice hers is a strawberry flavour and I wonder whether she's chosen it to match the colour of her blouse. As we walk back to our vehicles, I wonder about Grant Michaels again.

'Grant seems to be the odd one out in your group,' I say.

'I've never seen it that way but you're right in the sense that he likes different things to most of us. But's that's not necessarily a bad thing, is it?' We're standing in front of Candice's Subaru.

'Of course not. But if he hasn't got that much in common with you guys, why does he join you each year?'

'Probably because, before he was married, he got to see Fiona,' Candice says.

I nod. 'Want to come over?' I ask.

'Not now. I'm tired and I have stuff to do at home.'

I kiss her and watch her slide into the driver's seat. Then I walk to where I'm parked, a little miffed that she didn't join me at home.

I hadn't seen her for a week and I'm particularly horny. I guess I'll have to be patient.

Driving home, I wonder if there is any significance to Grant being involved with a group with whom he doesn't share anything except being at university with them many years ago. But then people have all different kinds of motivations.

THIRTY-ONE

A CAT FIGHT WAKES HER. Amanda looks at her phone to see the time. 6:50 am. She rolls over and tries to get back to sleep. Then she recalls that it's her new start here, in Sydney, at the Bondi police station. That motivates her to get up. After brushing her teeth, she dresses in a T-shirt, shorts and runners and goes for a walk to check out her environment and get some exercise.

The walk over, Amanda returns to her flat, small but cosy, and prepares for the day. Freshly showered and dressed in work clothes, she strides along Campbell Parade then turns into Curlewis Street and left into Gould Street.

Amanda reports to the Bondi Beach Police Station commander at eight-thirty Monday morning. Errol Harding, a tall sandy-haired man shakes Amanda's hand then walks her to the area inhabited by other members of the branch and points to a desk and chair for her to use.

'I understand, from talking to a colleague, that you'd been temporarily assigned to Parramatta Homicide Squad when you last worked in New South Wales,' says Harding when he's with Amanda in the centre of the office.

'That's right, sir,' Amanda says, 'I was assigned for one case and I haven't been advised whether I'm still needed. For now, I'm at your disposal.'

'Very good. Let me check with Police Command to make sure you're no longer required, and I'll let you know. Just have my PA, Ann, who's sitting over there introduce you to the others in the meantime.' Harding points to the dark-haired woman, in her fifties, walking back to her desk.

Amanda nods. 'Thank you, sir.' She places her bag on the desk, sits down, and opens one of the drawers to see whether it's empty. Having done that, she shuffles out of her cubicle to meet with Ann Parks who is now sitting outside Harding's office.

Parks takes Amanda around the station introducing her to her colleagues as well as showing her the kitchen and facilities.

Just as Amanda sits down at her desk ready to start the desktop computer, Harding asks her to come back into his office.

'Yes sir,' says Amanda.

'It appears the case you were on at Headquarters has not been concluded and the team would like you to return,' says Harding sitting back in his leather chair. 'You can report to them tomorrow. Today, get oriented to our operation here.'

'What should I do in the meantime?'

'Familiarise yourself with our local policies. Ann will guide you. See you when the murder case is over.' Harding returns to a piece of paper he has on his desk.

Amanda goes back outside and sits down. She's pleased to be going back to Hank's team but wonders whether Hank will be glad to see her.

That night, as she leaves the station wandering down Roscoe Street to Campbell Parade, Amanda is jubilant. She's set up in a new team, she has accommodation and she'll meet Hank Rockwell again.

On her walk along Campbell Parade to the Bondi flat she's secured in Beach Road, she glances at the beach and sees people in the water, swimming or body surfing. She stops off at a restaurant but decides not to eat out alone. She buys a Thai takeaway meal and consumes it in front of the television.

***

I arrive in the office on Tuesday morning later than usual. I parked close to Chatswood station and took the train to Parramatta. The sky is blue with a few wisps of white cloud floating by. I've not bothered getting a coffee which is a mistake. Now I'll be grumpy until I get some coffee. I head into the kitchen, not keen to substitute my usual Cappuccino with the brew that's available here. As I walk in, I see a familiar figure. The woman turns and I see that it's Amanda. It's an illusion, surely, I think. She's in Queensland and my mind must be confusing any gorgeous brunette with Amanda. But then she speaks.

'How are you Hank…I mean, boss?'

'Amanda,' I say to convince myself. 'It's you. I had no idea you were back.'

'Yes. I've been assigned to the Bondi Beach station. Got in on Saturday night.'

'Come into my office, would you?' I say, organising my coffee, with milk and half a spoon full of sugar.

Seated in my office, I gaze at her. She's as beautiful as ever, the many months in Queensland not having dimmed her radiance. Of course, my mind had made the vision of her fade but that's my mind. Out of sight, I've found, means the image gradually disappears. I'm nothing if not unsentimental. 'Well, how have you been?'

Amanda explains the situation with her mother, the illness, the death. 'So, I decided I wanted to live in Sydney where I've always felt comfortable. And I've been transferred to Bondi Beach due to the higher-ups arranging matters. Not that I'm complaining. Lovely change.'

'I'm pleased. It's nice to see you again. As for the Brent Morton case, we still have work to do. I must confess I've not come up with any great strategy to find our killer.'

'So, the five friends are all suspects?'

I can't say I have narrowed it down to one or two, so I have to agree with her. 'Would you please look at all the reports and the evidence again? With your break, you may come up with fresh ideas.'

'Of course,' she says, getting up and leaving.

I sit back and lace my fingers at the back of my head. What a pleasant surprise. But I can't take up with her again. I have Candice. It may prove a blessing in disguise. At least by having another girlfriend, I won't be tempted to have an inter-office affair which could be tricky to negotiate. But it will be good to have her around the place for another little while.

* * *

Amanda sits at her desk and pulls up the reports on the Brent Morton murder. But seeing Hank has distracted her, an altogether predictable outcome, nevertheless unsettling, she shuts her eyes and meditates for a moment. He seemed really happy to see her and she wonders whether he is keen to continue the relationship. But that has to wait. She begins to read the statements of the five surviving friends, key suspects to date.

Brent knew his killer; that is clear. There were no defensive wounds, no struggle. So that rules out strangers coming to the cabin. All the suspects stated they'd left the swimming pool area well before the time Morton was knifed. Which means, she figures, each one of them could also have easily returned to inflict the fatal strike. It comes down to determining who has most to gain. Or was it hate or jealousy or revenge? The women had all been hit on by Brent and may have wanted revenge. Why the men would want Brent killed is less clear.

Amanda begins to prepare a report for Hank Rockwell. She recalls as she types that Hank mentioned his theory that Grant Michaels may have had a reason to harm Brent. But, from everything she's considered, she can't agree with that assessment. The knife had also been examined and it was a common domestic knife, an eight-inch Chef knife, rather than a hunting knife which may have been brought in especially for the deed. Searches for each home of the five friends had been carried out. Each residence had been thoroughly examined by a police team and none contained a knife which was similar to the one used to murder Brent.

Amanda leans back to think.

THE VIEW IS ONE OF summer. Mums and dads paddling in the water with young children. Men and women walking dogs along the concrete walkway. The sun blazing outside but here, in the restaurant, the temperature is reduced to a comfortable one by the air conditioning.

I watch the activities outside as I wait for Candice to re-join me. We're at this luncheon to celebrate the Chief Constable's farewell. He's been in the police force for more than twenty-five years. I'm here because I'm in charge of a Homicide Squad team. The brass is here too but none of my team members have been invited to this fashionable and expensive Balmoral location. I gaze at the wharf-side café a hundred metres away. I've been to that venue, I recall, one more in keeping with my dining and entertaining preferences. This restaurant chosen by the Chief Constable's PA, I guess, is fancy and over-priced.

There are around a hundred guests. Seating has been organised so that the various ranks sit with their counterparts. Candice slides a loving hand across my shoulder as she comes back from the bathroom and sits down. Today she is looking magnificent in a sleek black dress but without it being too daring. It's not low-cut nor does it have a slit up the side as some of her other outfits which reveal too much skin. She looks as conservative as Candice can, just to please me and fit in. But this doesn't stop the stares. DS Graham Richards, a fifty-odd-year-old overweight cop, opposite us smiles when Candice is properly seated. His fat wife, Barbara, ignores us.

'Beautiful day,' says Richards, his eyes almost popping out of his skull.

'Yes,' says Candice, 'Are you keen on the beach?'

'Well, yes…,' says Richards.

'Don't lie,' snaps Barbara, 'You've never liked the beach. Your skin turns beetroot red.'

'Perhaps Graham enjoys peering out at the water,' I say, to rescue my colleague. I wonder whether he and his wife had a fight on the way here. She's obviously jealous of him talking with Candice so I diffuse the situation by suggesting to Candice to leave the restaurant and go for a walk.

'What a cow,' Candice says when we're outside.

I laugh. 'I understand why men want to chat to you and I understand Barbara's reaction. You can't help being so sexy.'

Candice squeezes my arm. 'You say such wonderful things. I hope I never lose you.'

We stroll along, slowly, eyeing the other pedestrians and dog traffic. The sun beats down, yet I find it pleasant, particularly with a soft breeze running off the water. All appears perfect for the day until we bump into another couple. I look back to apologise but can't believe what I see. Amanda and another woman.

'Sorry,' says Amanda. Then she realises who we are. 'What…' She leaves the sentence unsaid.

'Hi,' I say, startled and unable to gather my thoughts.

'This is Lisa,' Amanda says, introducing the fair skinned woman with a typical English complexion. She also has short straight blonde hair which she brushes aside when she smiles at us.

'Nice to meet you Lisa. We're at a work function today. Oh yes, please meet Candy,' I say, hoping I'm not sounding awkward. 'How come you're not walking along Bondi Beach, Mand…Amanda?'

Amanda glares at me. 'Lisa lives up the road in Mosman and I decided to pop over to catch up.'

'Right. Anyway, we'd better continue. See you.' I take Candice's hand.

We walk on and Amanda and Lisa walk past us and down towards the wharf. My stomach stirs a bit. Amanda looked unhappy. Was it because I hadn't asked her to the police function or was it because Candice was with me? What's done is done. I can't undo it. I'll have to take the flak from Amanda in the office.

'Wasn't that your partner?' Candice asks.

'Yes.'

'She seemed miffed, I'd say, if her facial expression was anything to go by.'

'Really? I hadn't noticed,' I lie. We carry on but return to the function after another fifteen minutes. The day has been partially spoiled for me, but it doesn't prevent me from inviting Candice back to my place.

* * *

Grey blankets the skies as I drive from Collaroy to a roadside parking spot, a fair distance from the usual train station I take when I decide to catch public transport. The grey matches my mood. I park and walk in a leisurely fashion a few blocks along Victoria Avenue to the Chatswood station. Using my Opal card, I pass through the barrier and head to the platform which will take me to Parramatta. Waiting, I wonder what the day has in store for me. Should I be more concerned about Amanda or the case which is now drifting along, the initial momentum gone? I've read Amanda's report which suggests that Candice, Fiona or Sally are the main suspects. I haven't discussed her reasoning or conclusion with her, as yet, and I hope to do so today.

On the train, I usually read. Today, however, I'm not keen to do that. I lean back and close my eyes. I think back to yesterday when the police farewell function had concluded, and I was at my house with Candice. When she was straddling me later that night, my mind flashed back to a movie, Basic Instinct I think, in which, during the final scene, the seductive female pulled out a knife from under the bed and stabbed the cop to have him come to an unpleasant climax. For a brief moment when Candice was riding me, I thought she may have been guilty of Brent's murder and that she got close to me as a tactic to prevent being found out. Killing me off might have been her end game.

But here I am, alive and kicking. As the train rattles through another station, I feel stupid for thinking that Candice would harm me. I'm getting paranoid, I think. That's no way to live. On my walk to the office, I buy a carton of Cappuccino, as usual. I place the coffee on my desk and get the computer activated. But before I have a chance to settle, Amanda walks in.

'How are you today?' I ask.

'Fine. You should be ashamed of yourself, sir,' says Amanda.

I see the stern expression on Amanda's face. If she were a thundercloud, she would burst. 'Sorry, what are you talking about?'

'Associating with a key suspect in a murder investigation. Surely that's a huge no-no, a serious conflict of interest, particularly in an unsolved murder case,' she says, glaring.

I wait for more, surprised she's not stamping her feet on the floor, like a spoiled four-year old. 'Take a seat,' I eventually say.

'No thanks. I've lost all respect for you.'

'Sit down,' I command. I'm not sure whether Amanda is annoyed that I'm seeing a suspect or dating another woman. Is jealousy driving her anger or is it purely professional? 'You are out of order. I understand your point of view, but I have analysed all aspects of this case and I'm confident Ms Berry is not the killer.'

Amanda looks at me, having taken a seat opposite me, her expression a fraction more subdued. 'I don't know how you can come to that conclusion.'

'What you don't know is that I've been dating Candice to gain information about that tragic night at the Hydro,' I say, hoping she will soften her attitude towards me.

'A likely story,' she says, her tone less hostile.

I sip some coffee. 'Alright, let's get all the suspects in here and we'll put them under pressure to see what falls out. You can be chief questioner of Candice Berry.'

'That sounds like a plan but how does that mitigate the effect of you dating that woman?'

'I don't know. I can't make you believe I've been working, admittedly unconventionally.'

'How would your superiors react if they knew?'

Amanda is angry, I know that now. I need to be careful. I could take her off the case, but she may just be angry enough to report me. 'To calm your concerns, I won't see Candice …'

'Candice!'

'That's her name. Anyway, I won't see her until this case is wrapped up. Satisfied?'

'Whatever you say,' Amanda says then gets up and leaves my office, lips tightened in a straight line.

Once Amanda has gone, I try to think how I can tell Candice of my decision. I'm going to keep my word, that's for sure. The last thing I am is a man without integrity. I know dating Candice could be seen by others as a betrayal of ethics, but I don't see it that way.

Now, I prepare for the interviews which I'll get Amanda to set up. Again, I read the statements of the five surviving friends and take some notes. Then, at eleven o'clock, I email Amanda and ask her to send me a schedule of arranged interviews.

THIRTY-THREE

THE DAY IS WARM, A slight breeze making it tolerable outside. I walk along the beach, sand squeezing between my toes. As I've taken my shirt off, having applied sunscreen earlier, in an attempt to stem sun damage, I appreciate being at one with nature. I'm aware Australia has one of the highest levels of skin cancer in the world and I want to avoid that particular disease. I reach home and whilst showering, I wonder why Amanda has called Mitch in for the first interview. From her notes, I understand she believes the three women had greater motivation to do away with Brent. Still, I guess we need to start somewhere.

I meet Amanda in my office at ten-thirty, thirty minutes before the scheduled time to meet with Mitch Norris. She is dressed in dark clothes, a pantsuit of some kind. She also reflects a dark expression, I think, her lips tight and avoiding eye contact.

'Have you studied the file on Norris?' I ask when she sits down.

'Yes. I'm fully prepared. Not only have I read his statements to date but also his background and comments from friends and family.'

I examine Amanda's face to see if there is any sign of hostility towards me, but she appears to be acting professionally. Professional perhaps but definitely unsmiling. If I detect she's going to disrupt the process because of her personal grievance towards me, I won't hesitate to remove her from the case. 'Okay, let's do it.'

'Are we playing good cop, bad cop?' Amanda asks.

'Let's see how it goes. We won't premeditate,' I say.

At five minutes after eleven, five minutes after Norris has arrived and been installed in the interview room, I follow Amanda into the small square space. She takes a seat and I take the chair to her right. I notice that the communication equipment is ready to be switched on. I nod to Amanda and she does the honours.

Mitch Norris looks entirely different from the time we met with him at the Hydro Majestic. He's wearing a dark suit, a white shirt, red tie, and cufflinks. His hair is slicked back, and he is clean shaven. His expression is neutral. He moves his broad shoulders back into the chair, appearing relaxed.

'Please state your full name for the recording, Mr Norris,' Amanda says.

'Mitchell Robert Norris.'

'Mr Norris, would you take us through the events of that night at the Hydro Majestic when Brent Morton died?' I ask.

'Okay but I don't understand why you want to discuss it now, so many weeks afterwards,' says Norris.

'We need to know as much as possible. You may now recall something that you passed over before. We're simply trying to be as thorough as possible,' I say. I don't mention that he's now not drunk, thus more coherent.

'Thinking back, I recall checking into the hotel in mid-afternoon. We, Sally and me, were given our room number and told where our room was. We took our luggage to the room and unpacked. Sally changed for the evening. I didn't bother. Is this the stuff you want to know?'

'Yes, Mr Norris, that's good,' confirms Amanda.

I wait for Norris to continue. It occurs to me that Norris, sober, is far more reliable. The detail is good as I'd speculated, and I hope he will continue in this vein until the story is over. 'I agree,' I say, nodding.

'We walked to the Boiler Room and met up with Brent and Candice. Grant and Fiona hadn't arrived at this stage. We had some drinks and talked about what's been happening since we last got together.' Norris leaned forward. 'Can I get some water?'

'Sure,' I say. 'Let me go. DC Walsh will keep you entertained while I'm gone.' I wander out, pleased for the break. I fill a plastic bottle with water, get a cup of coffee for myself and go back into the room. 'Okay, Mr Norris, the floor is yours.'

'Where was I? Oh yes, after having a few drinks, Grant and Fiona joined us.'

'What was the conversation about then?' I ask.

'Basically, the same but more about Grant and Fiona's year.'

'And what did Grant and Fiona say about their year?' I ask.

'Fiona mentioned moving in with Grant,' says Norris.

'And Grant?' I push him.

'That prig. Told us about his successes at work. The promotions he got and the money he made.'

'How did you guys react to that?' I continue. It appears to me that Mitch had little time for Grant.

'I didn't comment. I just let him tell us what a superior bloke he is. Brent laughed and asked him when he expected to be the company's CEO. The girls stayed quiet.'

'So, you guys resented him because he's more successful than you?' Amanda asks.

'I couldn't care less. Thought he was a jumped-up dick. And Brent wasn't his greatest fan either,' Norris says, taking another sip of water.

'Given Brent's attitude to Grant, would you think Grant had a motive to kill him?' I ask. I find it interesting that these so-called friends aren't as close as it would appear to an outsider.

Norris laughs. 'He doesn't have the guts. Can't imagine him killing anyone except by boring them to death.' Norris chuckles again, probably at his own joke.

I lean back and watch. I'm learning a lot more than before and now know that I've made the right decision to have all the friends come into Headquarters for a further interview. I glance at Amanda to see whether she has questions.

'What about the women?' Amanda asks, 'Can you contemplate any of them murdering Brent, given that he'd forced them into having sex?'

'Did he? News to me,' says Norris.

For a moment the room is quiet. Did Norris not know what his mate was like or is he playing us? I doubt Mitch would not know about Brent's activities as they were best friends but it's likely he's going to be loyal to his friend even in death. I guess it doesn't matter so I ask him to continue.

'Well, we decided at around seven o'clock to have something to eat. So, we wandered along to the dining room. Brent was chatting to me and Grant went along with the three ladies. We found a table for six and ate. Nothing of interest happened.'

'What were the seating positions?' Amanda asks.

Norris grimaces as if to say, who cares. But he says, 'Grant sat opposite Fiona, Sally opposite Candice in the middle and I was opposite Brent.'

'Go on,' I say.

'Nothing much happened at dinner. Do you want to know what we ate?'

'No. It's fine unless you overheard a plot to kill Brent,' I say, realising that Norris was accepting the interrogation in a light-hearted mode. I feel if he is relaxed, he may tell us something of real value. A slip may occur if he sees this as a joke. 'So, what happened next?'

'Do you mind if I remove my jacket? He asks.

'Go ahead,' I say.

Norris takes off his jacket and drapes it over the back of his chair. Then when he's sitting again, he says, 'Around nine o'clock we head off to the venue with the band. People danced and drank alcohol. Sally was keen to participate but I'm no dancer, so Brent asked her up. I don't object as they're friends and …'

'Did you know about Sally and Brent's past?' Amanda asks, obviously keen to make out Sally had a difficult history with Brent.

'Yeah. They're good now. They had an up and down relationship like most of us have. Anyway, I prefer a drink to strutting around on a dance floor and I couldn't wait for it to be over. We then go to Brent's cabin.'

'What time is this?' I ask.

'About eleven, I guess.'

I finish my coffee which is tepid now, something I hate. Usually, I toss that kind of coffee out and make another. But we're getting close to the part of the story which counts, and I don't want to stall proceedings. 'Did you all go together?'

'Brent, Sally and I headed off first. The others joined us there not long after. It was a warm night, so we drank beer and wine or whatever else we had. Brent had been tasked to supply the booze and we all agreed to chip in and contribute money. The drinks were in Brent's fridge.'

'Were you all inside the cabin?' Amanda asks, shifting in her chair a little.

'Yes.'

'Wasn't it cramped? Six adults inside a small room.'

'It was cosy,' Mitch says, looking strangely at Amanda. 'Have you never been close to someone in a confined space?'

To push on and get back on track, I say, 'What happened next. Did you go outside?'

'Yeah. Then Brent suggested we take our clothes off as it's hot and as part of a fun game. Nobody protests so we play a game where we take turns asking questions of the person next to us and if that person gets the answer wrong, they have to discard a piece of clothing. By this stage we'd all had lots to drink so inhibitions were greatly reduced. The winner of this game was Fiona, so she was spared taking off her thong. But she eventually did take it off when we went poolside to cool down. Some of us even did some swimming. I was out of it, so I was content to splash about.'

I sit back and observe Norris. Is he telling the truth? Why would they all agree to such a game? It's possible although I can't say my small circle of friends would agree to something like that. But then again, I'm not typical as I don't engage with friends all that much. I could ask Amanda later about her situation, but she may not share stories with me as I'm not in her good books right now. 'What happened next?'

Norris drinks the rest of his water. I turn to Amanda and ask her to get him another cup. She gets up without complaint and leaves the room. I stare at Norris, trying to figure out why his throat is dry. 'You can wait for DC Walsh to return but I suggest you tell us the truth.'

'Everything I've said is the truth,' he exclaims.

'Why would all the females agree to play the game, as you say?'

'You'd have to ask them.'

Amanda enters the room, placing one cup in front of Norris and another in front of her chair. 'Did everyone get into the water?'

'Eventually. Brent and I jumped in first, but all the others eventually dived in, to frolic and mess about.'

'You were all sober enough not to drown?' I ask.

'Yeah. Some of us went back into the cabin to drink and a couple didn't but I couldn't tell you who did and who didn't. At some point I went to my…I mean, Sally's and my cabin.'

'What time?' Amanda asks.

'I'm not sure, I was wasted.'

I look at my notes. 'In your original statement you said you were the last to get to Brent's cabin. How do you explain the way you recalled it this time?'

'At the Hydro, I wasn't with it the morning after. Still hung over. But since then, I've thought about it, and I have a clearer picture of the events.' Norris gulps some more water.

'You didn't mention the game in your original statement either,' I say.

'I was a bit embarrassed to be honest,' says Norris.

'And you can't recall an approximate time when you left Brent's cabin?' Amanda asks.

'Sorry. No real idea. But I wasn't the last to leave, that I can tell you.'

I glance at Amanda to see whether she has further questions. She doesn't appear to have any, so I suggest she turns off the recording equipment. I smile at Norris and say, 'Thank you for coming in, Mr Norris. You've been helpful.' I stand and so does Norris who pulls his jacket off the back of the chair and shrugs it on. He shakes hands with both of us and leaves.

'See me in my office in ten minutes, thanks,' I say to Amanda. On my way back to my office I get water from the kitchen.

Amanda comes into my office and sits in the visitor's chair, silently, as though she were a ghost. I look up from my file on Mitch Norris. 'Thoughts on the interview?'

'We got a more detailed version of the events on the night, but it didn't help us find a prime suspect,' she says.

'Interesting about the game they played. Nobody mentioned that previously, did they?'

'No. It's the first I've heard of it.'

'Did you think he was lying?'

Amanda crosses her legs and for a moment my mind goes back to our night at the Hydro. Today I haven't looked at her closely but now when I do focus and peruse her face, I see how beautiful she is. She shrugs. 'Hard to say.'

'Who's our next interviewee?'

'Sally at four this afternoon,' says Amanda.

'How are you holding up?' I ask, nor sure why I say this. Maybe I wanted to establish whether she has thawed a little.

'Fine,' Amanda says. She gets up and leaves the room.

THIRTY-FOUR

Sally

TODAY SALLY IS DRESSED IN a simple yellow and black striped dress with low heeled black shoes. Her blonde hair is tied back in a ponytail. She's early and she is shown to one of HQ's interview rooms by a colleague. Amanda and I have our notes with us as we enter the room at 4:02 p.m.

'Good afternoon, Mrs Norris,' I say, 'Would you like something to drink?'

'No thanks. Call me Sally, would you. I have kids calling me Mrs Norris all day long.'

Amanda sits down and starts the recording. 'Hi Sally,' she says, 'Did you have a good day?'

'Hectic. Some of the classes went well and others I'd rather forget. But the work-day's over now so I can cross that one off.'

'Sounds like you'd like a break from work,' Amanda says.

'Mitch and I plan to start a family in a year or so then I can have a break,' Sally says.

'So, you want to dive in and have your own trouble-makers,' I say.

'Something like that,' Sally agrees.

'I know this is boring,' I say, 'but we'd like you to go over the events at the Hydro on the night when Brent died.'

Sally moves her eyes up towards the ceiling, thinking. Then she speaks, levelling her gaze on me. 'Ok, I'm back to that night, a night I'd rather forget. Mitch was in an upbeat mood when we joined Brent and Candice for drinks. Not sure whether he was happy to see Brent or keen to have a beer. Then Grant, the perpetually late Grant, and Fiona arrive in their fancy designer clothes.'

'Sounds like you don't think much of them,' I say, pleased to uncover their dirty secrets.

'Fiona's okay but she got involved with Grant who has an inflated opinion of himself. Having said that, I get along with both of them and as we only see each other every now and then, there's no problem and there are no bad feelings towards each other.'

'So, you have seen Grant and Fiona at other times?' asks Amanda.

'Yes.'

'What about Mitch? Did he accompany you on those occasions?' I ask this as it was clear from talking to Mitch that he had little time for Grant.

'No, Mitch didn't join us. It was on weekends when I'd have lunch with Fiona and sometimes Fiona and Grant when Mitch was watching football or cricket,' says Sally.

'What time did you have dinner at the Hydro?' I ask, steering the topic back to the night in question.

'Just after seven. I remember checking my iPhone for messages after drinks and I saw the digital display as 7:03 p.m.'

Well, I thought, someone with a precise answer and it accords with her husband's estimation. 'What did you have for dinner?' I ask to throw her off a bit.

'Fish, I think, yes it was barramundi which was excellent. After dinner we all strolled to the Boiler Room where we listened to the band and some of us danced. I had a few dances with Brent and as I said before there was an idiot who wanted to spoil the night by arguing.'

'Did Brent talk to you on the dancefloor?' asks Amanda.

'Not really. He tried to hold me too close on one occasion and I asked him to release me. Then he said I was being paranoid and asked whether I was afraid of being molested.'

'What did you say to that?' Amanda continues.

'Nothing. I let it slide.'

'What time did you leave the Boiler Room?' I ask.

'It's the Boiler House where live music is played. We left there around nine then went to the swimming pool area and into Brent's cabin, just opposite the pool, where we had drinks. After a while we got sick of being inside and somebody suggested a dip in the pool, a few metres outside Brent's cabin.'

I wait for more, but Sally doesn't add any further details. 'What did you do in the cabin?'

'We chatted and drank,' Sally says.

'Did you play a game?' I ask, checking Amanda's reaction. I wonder whether she is aware that Sally's version of events at this point is different to her husband's.

'What do you mean?' Sally says.

'Mitch told us that you played a game whereby each of you had to remove an item of clothing if you answered a question incorrectly,' I say. I need to understand what the truth is and what isn't.

'Okay, there was a game as you say. Once we'd removed our clothes Brent suggested we parade ourselves in front of each other. It was harmless enough and the exhibition raised a few giggles. What was somewhat disturbing was that Brent asked us, at the end of the parade, to get a score from each watcher for the quality of our bodies.'

'How did you score?' Amanda asks.

'I can't remember. Stupid game. But we did go into the pool afterwards,' Sally says.

I twist in my chair. 'Why didn't you disclose this before?'

'I was embarrassed. Grown people flaunting their nakedness for approval from friends. I wouldn't expect this of my primary school students,' says Sally, scratching her arm.

'Did you check your messages when you left Brent's cabin to go to your room?' I ask.

Sally laughs. "No, not this time. I was tired and just wanted to go to sleep.'

'So, you had no idea what time you left Brent's?' Amanda asks.

'Not exactly but I thought it was just after one in the morning.'

'Did your husband go back with you?'

'Yes. He may not remember because he was wasted but I walked, and he staggered back. He crashed as soon as he fell onto the bed covers. I had to push him aside, so I could squeeze under the covers on my side. What a night?'

I nodded to Amanda to turn off the recording. 'Thanks for coming in Sally. Enjoy the rest of your day.'

Sally rises and walks out of the interview room, leaving Amanda and myself alone.

'What did you think?' I ask.

'Her account seems consistent with what others have said.'

I stand. 'Would you like a drink?'

'I don't know,' says Amanda, pushing her chair back and standing.

'It's not a date, just a drink with a colleague. Hopefully, we'll be able to brainstorm about the interviews to see if there are any cracks.'

'Okay. Let me get my bag.'

It's late afternoon and a storm is brewing. Inside the pub, we sit across from each other in a venue with few patrons, a beer before me and a white wine in front of Amanda. She is looking attractive despite wearing dark trousers and a white blouse but I'm not going to tell her as she'll assume I want to flirt rather than carry on the discussion about the case. 'Sally didn't say much about Brent. Do you think she's covering up?'

'Maybe. The friends all seem to have plausible stories,' Amanda says, touching the stem of her wine glass.

'We haven't reinterviewed all of them yet so it's early days. However, I can't see a drunk Mitch Norris going back to kill Brent, can you?'

'Unlikely,' Amanda says.

'Sally could have gone back, and Mitch wouldn't have known as he was wasted, according to her account,' I suggest.

'I guess that's possible unless they colluded and murdered Brent together.' Amanda drinks some wine.

I'm thirsty and finish my beer. 'Even I think that's far-fetched. How are you settling back here at Headquarters?'

'Fine. Didn't think you cared.'

'Why wouldn't I care? You left for Queensland and I thought you were gone for good.'

Amanda finishes her wine. 'Didn't take long for you to find somebody else.'

'It just happened,' I say, wanting to avoid any discussion of Candice. 'I'll get another round.' I walk to the bar. I hear the thunder and then I almost feel the heavy rain as it descends, so forceful it is. We may have to wait out the miserable weather, I imagine. Can't walk out in this so Amanda is stuck with me a while longer.

* * *

Amanda is also conscious of the weather outside. She remembers that night at the Hydro Majestic when she knocked on Hank's door. She also recalls her heart racing when his body touched hers and the excitement she felt as their physical connection developed. She watches as he stands at the bar, waiting for service.

She wants him back but feels powerless to shape his actions. Candice has the raw feminine appeal, something most men desire. Even for Hank who she thought might be different. She can't bring herself to forgive him. She knows she's irrational but doesn't care. Can't he see that she would be better for him than that bawdy wench?

She sees him returning with another wine and a beer and notes he isn't smiling. He places the glass of wine on the coaster in front of her.

'Lousy weather,' he says.

'Yes,' she says, wondering what he means.

'We might need to wait it out. But we don't have a room.'

Amanda glares at him. Is he teasing? What does he mean? 'It should pass soon.'

'Who are we interviewing next?'

Amanda tells him the schedule she set up.

THIRTY-FIVE

FIONA IS DRESSED IN SLIM-LINE white slacks accentuating her long legs, a flowery designed top and white low-heeled shoes. She sits upright as though there's a stick up her arse. I wonder whether she's always had such impeccable posture. She looks at us, awaiting a question. Amanda has turned on the recording equipment and waits for me to begin the session.

'Thanks for coming in Ms Harrison,' I say. 'How's your day been so far?'

'Busy. I've taken the afternoon off and a temp is substituting for me. How can I assist your enquiries, as DC Walsh suggested over the phone?'

'We'd like you to go over the activities of the night Brent Morton died. I've reread your original statement which is lacking in detail,' I say.

Fiona presses a finger against her temple before she speaks. 'It's been some time now, but I'll try. Grant and I were the last to arrive at the Hydro and we met the others for a drink before dinner. Grant and I had unpacked and we both made sure we had a tidy cabin first. Everyone at the bar seemed jovial and I thought it would be a fun night. After that, we left the bar and strolled to the min building. We got to the dining room around seven, I think, and Grant and I both ordered seafood. The group talked about plans for the weekend and different cuisines. But there was nothing we talked about which was contentious so none of us had a beef with Brent at dinner. Actually, he spoke with Mitch most of all, as I recall.' Fiona reaches for her plastic glass of water which she'd requested before the start of the interview.

Amanda says, 'It seems Brent and you weren't great friends.'

'We weren't enemies either and none of us had reason to do him harm,' Fiona responds.

'Didn't he sexually assault you when you were at university?' Amanda persists.

'That was ages ago and I'd forgotten all about it.'

'Most women don't get over something like that,' Amanda continues.

'He didn't rape me. He was frisky and fresh and manhandled me a bit, but I fought him off. I didn't let it concern me at the time and I haven't held a grudge.'

'How did Grant take it?' I ask.

'He doesn't know. I didn't think it was something I should reveal to him and I'd appreciate it if you'd keep it to yourselves,' Fiona says. She sips more water.

I nod and look at Amanda. Does she want to pursue this line of questioning? She certainly has the view that Brent was a sexual predator and that that was his undoing. But Amanda stays silent. 'What happened next?' My purpose is to align their timing and stories.

'We go to where the live band is playing and, initially, we sit and listen and have some drinks. Brent gets up and dances with Candice. After a short time, Candice returns to join us, and Brent gets Sally to dance. He gets into an argument with another fellow on the dancefloor, but it doesn't turn physical.' Fiona pushes her short blonde hair back and frowns. 'At this stage, the events kind of blur. Grant and I got up for one dance, but whether it was before the skirmish, or after, I can't recall.'

'Do you need a break?' I ask.

'No, no, I'm fine. Somehow the next thing I remember is being at Brent's cabin, the one closest to the pool. Someone passed around weed and we drank, but I can't hold my liquor so I tried to confine it to one or two gins.'

'Did that work?' asks Amanda.

'More or less,' Fiona says.

I wait for her to talk about the game they played but she talks about going into the pool, naked. When she's finished her account, saying Grant and she left around one o'clock in the morning, I ask about the game.

'Well we did play a stupid game, but it only happened because we were inebriated. I'm sure it wouldn't have happened otherwise, and it was the first time we had been together in that way.'

'You mean naked?'

'Yes. On our previous annual reunions, we'd always kept our clothes on.'

I'm keen to get up and stretch but that's not possible now so I simply roll my shoulders a little, to get the blood flowing. 'Who suggested the game?'

'Brent did,' says Fiona. 'He was enjoying his smoke, the weed, and looking very relaxed.'

Amanda asks, 'Would this game and the nakedness have intimidated anyone, causing them to want to exact revenge?'

Fiona laughs. 'I doubt it. We were all pretty laid back at this stage. The booze and marijuana, as well as the late hour, played its part.'

'What happened when you got back to your cabin?' I ask.

'We went to sleep. We were too tired for anything else.'

'Did Grant also go to sleep?' I want to make sure he has an alibi.

'Yes. We were both tired.'

'Thank you, Ms Harrison, you've been most helpful,' I say.

She stands, checks that her clothes are in order and moves towards the door. As she opens the door, I ask, 'Does Grant go out without you much?'

Fiona turns around, 'Not a lot. Sometimes. Why do you ask?'

'No reason. You two seem very much in love.'

She smiles. 'We are.' She leaves.

'What was that about?' asks Amanda.

'As I've told you before, I like to ask questions out of left field.'

Amanda doesn't respond.

'We see Grant at five, do we?'

'No, he texted while we were interviewing Fiona. He's caught up, he said, so he postponed the meeting until tomorrow,' says Amanda.

'Did you remind him, that this is a murder enquiry?' I ask, annoyed. Who did this trumped-up idiot think he is?

'Umm, no I thought it would be okay. I didn't know there was a deadline.'

I grunt but discontinue the subject. Instead, I say, 'Did you get home without drama yesterday?'

'Yes, most of the storm had passed when I left.'

* * *

Grant Michaels is a slender fellow. He wears a tailored dark pin-striped suit and as he strides towards us, I sense he is irritated. He is late. Perhaps he thought we should have gone to meet in his offices. Amanda smiles at him and leads him into the interview room. I let them walk in first to take their seats, but I wander in slowly. I watch Grant fiddle with his red tie and smooth down his white shirt. I wonder how he would react if someone spilled red wine over his immaculate appearance. Would he take it on the chin or have a minor heart attack?

After the recording device has been set up, I pull out my chair and sit down. 'Thanks for coming in Mr Michaels, I trust you're able to spend a little time with us without an urgent call for your services.'

'I'm here. What else do you want? You have my statement. So, how much more do you need?'

I don't tell him that we will pursue our enquiries until we find the murderer. 'You're right. You did prepare a statement. But we'd appreciate your recollection now, now that your memory of the events may have changed."

'That's correct Mr Michaels,' says Amanda, 'we're following up to ensure we have all the information accurately recorded.'

Grant frowns. "Okay,' he says, as he moves his body forward, hands spread out on the table. 'After checking in around five o'clock, I called Mitch then Fiona and I met the gang for drinks at the Salon du. After a couple of drinks, I stopped having alcohol and had some water. After our drinking session, we wandered over to the Wintergarden Restaurant and dined. Later we took a swim at the pool. Fiona and I got to bed at one o'clock.'

I noticed he didn't mention the walk with Fiona, nor did he talk about the game in Brent's cabin. Is it an oversight, I wonder? I decide to attempt something bizarre. 'Are you a homosexual?' I use the term deliberately. Not 'gay' but 'homosexual'.

It seems like the air has gone out of the room. I sense Amanda's eyes on me. Is she appalled? Grant's eyes bore into mine, murderous fury in them if I read them correctly. His hands bunch up a fraction. He wants to punch me, I know. If we weren't being filmed and recorded, I'm sure he would do so.

'I'm not but what has that to do with anything?' Grant's hiss is undeniable.

Amanda says, 'DS Rockwell has been under pressure. I'm sure he didn't mean anything by his comment.'

I have to smile to myself. Amanda seems to be protective of this man. But it doesn't concern me or stop me from saying, 'I'm curious because we've seen you go to some gay pubs in Oxford Street.'

'You've been following me?'

'This is a murder enquiry should I need to remind you again and we have to cover all angles. We strongly believe one of you, one of the five of you going to the Hydro that weekend when Brent was killed, is guilty.' I await a response.

Grant remains silent. Then after a moment he says, 'Is that all? I need to get back to work.'

'Not so fast. We've barely started. Give us the details of activities when you were in Brent's cabin,' I say firmly, so that he understands he won't be going anywhere, until I am satisfied he's told us everything.

He explains about the game, the drugs and drink and finally how they all ended up in the pool. His story matches with Fiona's, so I turn to Amanda to see whether she has anything to add. She shakes her head.

'You're free to go Mr Michaels,' I say after allowing another minute to pass.

Once Grant has gone, Amanda turns to me. 'What was all that about?'

'I've been searching for a motive. The women have had bad sexual experiences with Brent, and I wondered whether Grant had also had such an experience.'

'That's a long shot,' she says.

'It is, I grant you, but we need to examine the possibility.'

Amanda looks at me. 'Are you homophobic?'

I twist further to eye her fully. 'I didn't think so. If Grant is gay, he's hiding it. Think about it. He's ultra- neat, dresses fashionably, lives with Fiona who looks boyish and he's extremely sensitive.'

'That doesn't make him gay.'

'True. So why does he visit gay establishments?'

Amanda doesn't debate the issue any further. 'Our last interviewee is scheduled for tomorrow at noon.'

THIRTY-SIX

I wake to the sound of hail on the roof. Sliding out of bed, I check to see that all the windows are shut. Peering outside through the glass-panelled back door, I watch as nature unleashes a force which can't be tamed. And as I do so, I wonder whether Amanda and Candice will play nice or react like the storm outside, turbulent, and unrelenting. Suddenly I hear metal against metal, no doubt a road accident. I walk to the front and see two vehicles on the road. But it's only a minor collision and the drivers are standing in the pouring rain and hail to confront each other over the damage. As I'm not in the traffic division, I'm not getting involved, so I walk into the bathroom to get ready for another day on the Brent Morton murder case.

When I arrive, Amanda asks me whether she can talk to me. I invite her into my office. She is dressed in a pin-striped business suit and high heels. She looks great and I can only surmise it's because she's going to interview Candice today. Seeing her rival across the table may well bring out emotions which will be anything but pleasant.

'What's on your mind?' I ask. I've worn my dark suit today as well.

'I was hoping that I might be allowed to question Candice without your presence, given the conflict issue,' she says, somewhat shyly.

"

I lean back, watching her eyes and general expression which seems neutral. I know she has an agenda, but I don't detect any malice. What she's said makes sense. After all, if I joined the interview, Candice may think the session is not serious. This wouldn't be acceptable to anyone, me included. 'Okay, I'll get Alex to join you. Is that acceptable to you?'

'Of course, that would be great. Thank you.'

Amanda leaves. Before Candice arrives, I set myself up in the viewing room, making sure the audio is working perfectly. I don't want to talk to Candice until the interview is concluded. Just as I'm seated, ready to watch and listen, a knock on the door disturbs me. The door opens, and a young woman, a recently joined constable, comes in and hands me an evidence bag with a mobile inside.

'I was asked to give this to you,' she says. She is in her mid-twenties, I guess, with dark hair and of mixed European and Asian features. Her accent is pure Aussie.

'What is it?' I ask.

'I was told it came from the Hydro Majestic. The hotel management handed it in to their local police station when a guest occupying the room where a murder occurred recently, I was told, left it at reception.'

'What about it?'

'That's all I know, sir.'

'Thanks,' I say. When I return to my seat in front of the two-way mirror, I see Candice taking her seat. Today she's wearing a conservative grey skirt and white frilly blouse, but it doesn't hide her curvaceous body.

Amanda and Alex arrive a moment later with Alex doing recording duties. Amanda starts proceedings, introducing herself and Alex and advising the recording of the time, day and date.

'Thanks for coming in, Ms Berry,' says Amanda, after having offered Candice a drink which was declined.

'Where's DS Rockwell?' asks Candice.

'He's not available,' says Amanda, a consummate professional.

'Okay. So how can I help you?' asks Candice, pushing back her red hair. Today her hair looks vibrant, a richer red sometimes worn by the actress, Jessica Chastain. I presume she'd been to the hairdresser in the last day or so. It matches her red lips.

'Would you run through the events of the weekend when Mr Morton was found murdered, please.'

'I told you before. Didn't you take notes?' Candice says in an exasperated tone.

'We did, but you may have thought of something or remembered something else since the initial statement. This is routine, I can assure you,' says Amanda.

Candice looks directly at Amanda for a moment before focussing on the table. 'Very well. Brent and I went back years, in our relationship, to our university days. But I didn't particularly like him then. Anyway, he offered to drive me up to the mountains on this occasion in his big loud car, a Hilux. It was new and he wanted to show it off. I thought it was a kind gesture, so I accepted. We arrived at the hotel some time near five o'clock as I recall. We checked in, each of us getting our own room. Our relationship at this point, ever since university, was purely platonic.'

'Why didn't you share the same room?' asks Alex. 'As friends perhaps.'

'Over the years our relationship changed. He has made inappropriate passes at me, grabbed me and so on. I just didn't like it and I told him I wouldn't sleep with him,' Candice says looking at Alex.

I wait, watching the three players in front of me through the glass. I'm intrigued and I feel like I'm seeing a play unfolding before me.

'You hated him, didn't you?' Amanda says.

'What?' Candice turns her gaze back to Amanda. I can sense the two women don't like each other. Their stares are like daggers, sharp, deadly.

'You hated Brent because he raped you,' says Amanda with emotion.

'He was forceful, but he didn't rape me. I would have reported it if he had.'

The two women end their staring match after a few more seconds and Candice proceeds with her story. I half listen as she tells the events of the evening leading up to the group encounter in Brent's cabin.

Amanda breaks the monologue. 'Did everyone in the group get stoned or drunk?'

'Only Mitch was visibly drunk,' says Candice.

'So, the rest of you were coherent and could have managed to stab Brent,' continues Amanda.

'Why would we?'

'I don't know. All the females had motive.'

'That's rubbish,' says Candice.

'No, it's not,' says Amanda.

The women glare at each other. I can just imagine the two of them having a catfight if Alex wasn't present. The image of them pulling hair, rolling on the floor, and wrestling, hitting each other with soft blows forces itself into my mind. My imagination runs riot. For a moment I lose track of the actual scene, but I'm brought back to the present when Alex talks.

'Who do you think might have murdered Brent?'

Both women break their determined stares and Candice says, 'I don't know. That's your job, isn't it?'

'You were the last person to leave Brent's cabin, according to your initial statement, that's right, isn't it?' Amanda is like a terrier with a bone.

'That's right. But he was alive when I left.'

'What time was that?' Amanda peers at a piece of paper in a notebook in front of her.

'Around one forty-five.'

Not much more happens. It seems like Amanda has run out of spite. The two officers conclude the interview and Candice leaves without shaking anyone's hand or saying anything. I can tell she's pissed off.

'What's your conclusion?' I ask.

Amanda and I are enjoying a cup of coffee in my office. It's coffee from the kitchen so it's not great. Amanda is sitting on the visitor's chair, leaning back, looking tired.

'Difficult to catch anyone out. But I'm sure one of Brent's five friends committed the crime,' she says, staring at her cup, probably debating whether to drink it or pour it down the sink when she leaves my office.

'I agree but which one is the question,' I respond.

'Candice has the most compelling motive.'

'Why do you say that?'

'Her history with Brent has been the most chequered.' Amanda leans forward and takes her cup from the edge of my desk. Sips from it and returns the cup to the same spot.

'Maybe but that's hardly convincing,' I say to keep the discussion moving.

'I can't blame her, in a way. The guy was a creep.'

'Creeps should be murdered then?' I ask. I find it difficult to suppress a grin.

Amanda doesn't respond. She has more coffee as do I. The conversation seems to have come to an end. I wonder whether I'm considered a creep, now that I've taken up with Candice. And would Amanda find my death justifiable?

'What now?' Amanda asks.

'We'll have to rethink our approach. For the time being, let's take a break. Do you want to stay on the case here or go back to Bondi?'

'Why do you ask? I'd like to see it through,' Amanda says.

'You disapprove of my activities, so I thought you'd like to be where I'm not,' I say, watching her face for any tell-tale sign of deception.

'I'm a professional. What you do in your private life, even though it breaks the rules, is your concern, not mine.'

'Okay. Let's get back to work. Why don't you analyse the revised statements to see if there are notable inconsistencies?'

CHATSWOOD CHASE FOOD HALL IS awash with people. Most tables are occupied. There are all sorts of nationalities here with a predominance of Asians. Does this place remind them of Hong Kong, I wonder? I buy a coffee and a muffin and look around for a spot. I find a seat when a couple leave a table. I sit down and contemplate life. It's unfair, I figure. Not long ago I had nobody with whom I felt compatible. Now, I like, maybe even love, two wonderful women. Yet there are complications. With this situation going on, I find concentrating on the criminal cases for which I'm responsible difficult.

I watch the movements around me. There are couples sitting together, some chatting, some eating, others viewing their phones. Families also take up much space, parents getting their children to sit down at the table and focus on their food or drink. A contained chaos. Then there are single individuals strolling about with trays of fast food searching for a place to enjoy their lunch.

Then I see him, Russell from Forensics. He is tall and wiry, with a greying moustache. He also has a full head of unruly salt and pepper hair. I've known Russell for well over a decade and he and I have enjoyed each other's company over some beers. Always professionally. Never social, outside of work. But today we are meeting here at Chatswood Chase as Russell had medical appointments in the morning and one in the afternoon so there was no point him travelling to Parramatta to see me when he lives in Chatswood.

We shake hands when he gets to my table. He is as tall as I am as I stand to pump flesh. He sits down, casting a curious eye over my muffin.

'Coffee?' I ask.

'No thanks. I was going to talk to you in the office tomorrow, but I've just received results of our investigation and thought you'd like to get the information as soon as possible.'

'I appreciate it,' I say leaving the rest of my muffin on the paper plate.

'As you know a phone was handed in by a guest from the cabin previously occupied by Brent Morton to the Hydro Majestic management. They forgot about it for a while then passed it on to the local police station. Who passed it on to us, eventually, although I can't figure why it took so long for anyone to find it. So, it's been out of circulation for a while.'

'Okay,' I say, hoping he would get to the point.

'We discovered a partial recording on it. What's interesting is that it includes a gasp consistent with someone being stabbed.'

'Really? Were words also recorded?'

'Some.'

'What were they?'

'My team has sent a full transcript to your department.'

'Ok, to whom in particular?'

'Your squad PA, I think. Anyway, I have to shoot off. Perhaps we can catch up for a drink next week?' Russell stands and I stand, and we shake hands.

'Of course,' I say, 'Thanks for the intel.'

I watch Russell stride away. Then I resume consuming my muffin. Rather than calling the office and having the details sent to my email, I decide to wait until later to obtain the information.

I'm hot so I take my jacket off and hang it up on the hanger behind my door. It was the brisk walk from the station, I figure. I check my emails. My PA has done the right thing and sent the information to me. I read the transcript. Having read it, I call Amanda on the intercom to invite her into my office.

Amanda is dressed in her conservative pin-striped suit which suits her conservative expression. It reminds me of a former English high school teacher of mine who never smiled. 'Yes, sir,' she says as she enters.

'Take a seat please, Amanda.'

She complies, places one leg over the other, and folds her hands in her lap.

'I've just read a transcript of a phone recording and I thought we should get the phone and hear it together. It may tell us who the culprit is.'

Amanda looks a little confused. 'Why didn't we get this before now?'

'That's a long story. Should I read the message to you first?'

'Please.'

'There are two speakers. The first one is Brent but the second one could be any of the five others. Okay?'

'Right,' says Amanda.

I read out the transcript. 'Brent -What are you doing back here? Other- Wanted to get something off my chest. Brent- really? Why didn't you talk to me before? Other – I didn't want to start an argument in front of everybody. Brent – you sissy, Doris. Other – what are you doing with that phone? Brent – none of your business… hey what…'

'That's it?'

'Yes, that's all we have. I can only guess the visitor grabbed the phone and tossed it and it stayed hidden until the next guests occupied the room.'

'If we hear the voice, we'll know who the visitor was and that should tell us who the murderer is,' says Amanda.

'That's the theory. I'll arrange for the phone to be sent to us and then I'll call you in. Okay?'

'Okay. I'm excited, aren't you?'

I sit up a little straighter. 'I'm not going to get ahead of myself, but it looks promising.'

Amanda and I are in an office which has been set up to listen to the phone recording. We're seated and I have the control to switch on the audio. One of our tech people has arranged for the voices to be magnified. All we need to do is press a button and then the mystery will be solved. I'm wondering what could go wrong. It seems too simple, too good to be true. But perhaps once in a while, we get a break. I press the button.

The first voice I assume is Brent's. I have to assume this as I've not met the man nor heard him speak. Then the second voice comes on and it's hard to hear whether it's male or female. We continue the recording and by the end of it we're no wiser.

We repeat the process. And again. And again.

'That was a gigantic waste of time,' I say, frustrated by the lack of clarity. This should have been a slam dunk but has turned out to be nothing of substance. We knew there had been somebody who'd gone back into Brent's cabin. We knew Brent had been stabbed. All we've learned from the recording is that Brent was talking to somebody called Doris.

'Can the technical department make the voices clearer?' asks Amanda.

'Who knows? I somehow doubt it, but we can try. So, who would have been called Doris?'

Amanda shrugs. 'I don't know. I don't recall anybody mentioning that nickname.'

I peer at the door behind Amanda as somebody knocks. 'Come in.' I say.

'Sorry sir,' says Alex. 'Just letting you know I've been called to another job.'

'That's fine. See you later,' I say.

'If the name was Doris,' Amanda says, 'Doesn't it suggest that the killer is a woman?'

'Perhaps.'

'Perhaps?' Amanda is clearly exasperated.

'Let's get a cup of coffee outside of the building and we'll formulate a strategy,' I say.

Amanda doesn't argue. We find a favourite café of mine and settle into seats, awaiting our order. 'Thoughts?' I ask.

'Somehow we need to talk to the five people again and see whether anyone can tell us who Doris might be.'

'The name always reminds me of Doris Day,' I say.

'Who?'

'Have you never watched a Doris Day and Rock Hudson movie?'

'Afraid not.'

'Okay. You talk with the boys and I'll do the girls,' I say.

'So that you can meet up with Candice, I assume,' says Amanda.

'Let's not argue about this. We have a job to do and I'm still the boss, as far as I recall.'

'Yes sir,' says Amanda, her tone betraying a sarcastic bent.

Amanda sits at her desk, brooding. She hadn't meant to annoy Hank, but she couldn't help herself. She didn't think she was jealous but then, she didn't know for sure. It grated on her that, as soon as she was out of the picture, he'd found somebody else, another woman. So soon. It was almost disrespectful. He hadn't kept in touch with her when she was in Queensland or at least she would have been warned. It was a shock when she came across him in Balmoral with that Candy trollop. But now she has to get on with life. She thought, once she arrived back in Sydney, that she might reconnect with Hank. She really felt there was something good between them.

She stares at the computer screen, unfocused. Then somebody comes alongside. It's Jeff.

'What's up Amanda, you look as though you're carrying a world of worry on your shoulders?'

'Sorry, just deep in thought about a case,' Amanda says. She smiles and Jeff moves away. At least, Amanda thinks, she can talk to Mitch and Grant, so much better than talking to the women. She realises she hates the women because they were weak. Allowed themselves to get involved with a bully like Brent. A true misogynist.

Amanda gets back to work and arranges to see the men at convenient times. She hopes Hank will do the same with the women, professionally.

I enter the café in the Queen Victoria Building, close to the statue in Park Street. I take a seat, my back to a window, as I can't see any sign of Sally. By my watch, the time is ten-twenty and we've agreed to meet here so that the discussion won't feel like an interrogation. I order coffee. Just as it arrives, Sally walks into the café from the street entrance. She's wearing a green dress which is short to reveal toned legs. The kind of toning one gets from working out at the gym.

'Hi,' she says. She sits down opposite me. She has a view of the foot traffic outside.

'No problem getting time off from school?' I ask.

'No, I needed to get some things done in the city, so it works out fine.'

'Tea or coffee?'

After Sally's tea has been served and we'd dispensed with some small talk, I can get down to business. 'How well do you know your friends, the ones who went to the Hydro?'

'Pretty well, I'd say. Obviously, I don't know their intimate secrets but otherwise I'd imagine I know them well enough. Why?'

'Let's see how much you know. Does the name Doris mean anything to you?'

Sally frowns. She stares beyond me to the sunny vista outside. She turns her attention back to me. 'I don't relate the name to anyone I know.'

'You've never heard it used as a nickname for someone in your group?'

'No. Doris, it doesn't make sense. I don't believe that either Candice or Fiona have that as a middle name. And I certainly don't.'

We finish our drinks then go our separate ways.

'How did you go?' I ask Amanda when we meet in the office.

'Mitch has no clue about the name. And Grant is overseas on business, so I won't be able to contact him for a couple of days.'

'Okay,' I say, 'Not much we can do about that. Not looking good, I must say.'

'Would you like me to meet with one of the women?' Amanda asks.

'Sure. You check out Fiona's take on it. I've already set up a time with Candice.'

'Alright,' says Amanda, eyeing me oddly.

It's a Saturday and I'm in the middle of tidying my place. Putting items left around the lounge and kitchen in their proper places. Finally, at 10.22 a.m. I'm finished. I shower then change into comfortable jeans and a dark T-shirt. I even shave, something I don't normally do on weekends unless I'm going out on a date or to a function or party. But I'm expecting Candice soon and I want to appear reasonably respectable.

I didn't tell Amanda I would be interviewing Candice at home. I thought it would allow Candice to relax and that she would open up more easily. Of course, if I've misjudged the situation and Candice is the killer, then I could be in danger myself. She might have a small pistol or knife in her purse and strike me. But I'm arrogant enough to think I'd be equal to the threat and that I'd prevail, somehow.

Precisely at eleven, the doorbell chimes. I run my hand over my head and walk to the door, a little apprehensive. I haven't rehearsed how to introduce the topic, so I'll have to wing it. Bad police procedure I know but at this late stage, there's no option. I open the door and standing in front of me is Candice in heels and shorts and a blouse which reveals a deep cleavage. I swallow, wondering if I'm up to continuing the interrogation without compromising my good intentions.

'Please come in,' I say. I let her pass by me, her fragrance floral, and she stops a few feet inside.

She turns and says, 'Hello.' Then she reaches up and pulls my head down a little and kisses me full on the lips.

I don't resist. For a moment, a very small moment, I'm confused, not sure why I've invited Candice over. But it all comes back, like somebody with a sudden bout of Alzheimer's, getting over the flash of incoherence. 'Can I get you something to drink?' I ask.

'Coffee would be nice,' she says. 'You didn't say why you wanted me to pop over so early.'

'Take a seat. I'll make coffee and then all will be revealed.'

'Sounds exciting. I hope I like this game.'

As I make two cups of coffee, I try to think of a plausible strategy. But nothing comes to mind. I carry the cups to the lounge, noting that Candice has dropped her shoes on the carpet, and she has wrapped her legs under her bottom. 'Here you are. White no sugar, right?'

'What a memory,' says Candice. 'Now why have you asked me over so early? I'm more than keen to see you tonight.'

I place both cups on the coffee table between us and I sit on a black leather chair opposite the sofa. 'Doris,' I say, watching her facial features closely.

'What? Can't you remember my name or are you seeing somebody else? And we're not even in bed,' Candice says, her tone almost hysterical.

'Nothing like that. Calm down. I was testing you,' I say, somewhat relieved that she didn't respond recognising 'Doris' as her nickname.

'Testing for what?'

'Look Candice, I've wanted to ask you about something which would help our investigation. I'm sorry to do it this way but I also wanted to see you. Today you're so beautiful, I almost forgot why I asked you over,' I say, watching to see whether she's still incensed at me for calling her the wrong name.

'I see. That's pretty low,' she says.

'I know. Anyway, getting back to the investigation, I need to ask you whether Brent ever called anyone 'Doris' either as a person or as a nickname.'

Candice stretches out and then puts her feet on the carpet. 'Let me think. Something is stirring in the back of my mind. Don't you be sarcastic now.'

I sip my coffee. 'I wouldn't dare,' I say.

She smiles at me and I sense the worst is over. Unless she's a great actress and she's about to pull out a gun from somewhere. But this is impossible as her small, elegant purse wouldn't be able to conceal anything like that. 'I do recall Brent laughing at something he did in high school. But what was it? I can't think. It might come to me later. Why don't we go to bed? It's been so long.'

I'm tempted but I told Amanda I wouldn't. Then Candice moves over to me and sits on my lap, her huge breasts level with my mouth. I give in, justifying my behaviour on the basis of jogging Candice's memory. So, I pick her up and transport her to the main bedroom. I had only made the bed half an hour ago but I'm not going to let that impede the investigation. I toss her on the bed. We remove our clothes in haste. The love making doesn't last long as lust takes over.

Later, snuggled against her, in a spooning position, Candice says. 'It's come to me.'

'What has? The meaning of life?'

'No silly, the Doris thing.'

I wait.

'Brent once told me that he used to tease blokes in high school. The ones he thought were a little odd or prissy. Well Grant fitted that description as far as he was concerned, and Brent ended up calling him a poofter. Then to be creative he called him Doris.'

'Why?'

'Because Doris Day would play opposite Rock Hudson who turned out to be gay. And Brent thought it was a hoot that a gay man would pretend to be the lover of Doris Day. So, by calling Grant 'Doris' it implied he was the lover of homosexuals.'

'I see,' I say, ecstatic with this piece of information. I also feel that my method of extracting this information was creative, totally justifiable in the war against crime. Others may not see it like that but who am I going to tell.

In the early afternoon, Candice leaves my house, satisfied with the events of the day too, it seems. I don't ask whether she's had a good time. I figure she'd tell me if she hadn't. She's that kind of woman.

THIRTY-EIGHT

AMANDA AND I ARE ON our way to Grant's house. It's Sunday and we know Grant is now back from his overseas business trip, according to Fiona who advised Amanda yesterday. Amanda told me that she tried to set up a meeting for Monday, the following day, but Grant said she should come to his house today as he was due to depart again on Monday for another overseas business trip. She'd agreed, somewhat reluctantly as she wanted to interview him at the station. I told her I wanted to join her, and she hadn't objected.

As we arrive at Grant's Watsons Bay residence, I see a vehicle with Fiona in the driver's seat, heading away. Amanda and I climb the stone stairs of the white two storey house. At the top of the stairs, I press the bell. A moment later, the door opens and Grant smiles but when he sees me it fades. No doubt he thought he would be seeing Amanda by herself. And what did he have in mind? I wonder whether he would be tempted to make a move on her. But I doubt it. She is a model of goodness. He waves us inside.

The place is luxurious when compared to my modest abode, not that I'm particularly unhappy with my beachside apartment. But to some, a chandelier, white drapes, paintings by original artists, leather sofas and armchairs would seem heavenly. Personally, it's too fussy for me. The lounge contains too many cushions and ornaments for my liking. But I like the huge bookcases and the array of books neatly compiled. I look at Amanda and note that she is impressed.

Grant invites us to sit in any of the three comfortable chairs or the sofa. I select an armchair opposite the sofa which Amanda prefers. The room is huge. He asks whether we'd like a drink, a real drink, not coffee or tea.

'Water would be fine,' says Amanda.

I don't mention we're on duty, but I say water is good for me too. I see that even in his own home, Grant is dressed elegantly. Collared striped shirt and freshly pressed grey slacks. I wonder whether he's dressed in starched pyjamas when in bed. Does he get naked with Fiona or do they simply cuddle and talk about current affairs? Or gossip about friends, a more likely scenario.

Grant leaves the room and heads to the kitchen. Moments later, he reappears with a tray which he places on the glass coffee table. He places a glass of water in front of me and one in front of Amanda and himself. He also puts a plate on the coffee table. It contains cheese, crackers, and a knife to cut off a portion of the hard cheese. He sits next to Amanda, turns to her and asks, 'You said you wanted to chat. What about?'

Amanda turns to her right and says, 'A phone was found in Brent's cabin.'

'Okay,' says Grant, 'What's that got to do with me?'

'Have you ever heard of the name 'Doris'?' asks Amanda.

'Doris!' Grant pulls his face in a sort of contorted scowl. 'No, what's the name supposed to mean?'

I haven't disclosed to Amanda what happened in my meeting with Candice and I'm enjoying this scene with Grant acting innocent. Rather than spoil the moment, I await Amanda's response.

'We're trying to find out. It's strange. It may not mean anything.'

Grant smiles, satisfied he's in the clear. 'So, you found this name on his phone? Where did you find it?'

'No,' says Amanda, 'we discovered a muffled recording.'

'Oh! How bizarre.' Grant takes the serrated knife and cuts off some cheese which he places delicately on a thin wafer.

'You're Doris, aren't you Mr Michaels?'

Grant almost chokes on his biscuit. 'What?'

Amanda looks at me, wide-eyed and confused. She knows I think Grant is the culprit and probably believes I'm pushing him for no legitimate reason. She's about to say something but I raise my hand to silence her.

'Brent called you Doris at school, didn't he?' I say.

'That's rubbish. I don't know where you get this,' he says, waving the knife at me.

'It's true though, isn't it?'

'You have no proof,' he says.

'Candice told me. You were teased at school. You were called a homo, weren't you?'

With sudden swiftness, Grant with his left arm pulls Amanda towards him and points the knife at her throat, using his right hand. 'You have no idea of the torment that man caused me.'

'I understand,' I say, holding my palms up in a placating manner, 'but threatening Amanda won't help you. Put the knife down.'

'Toss me your handcuffs,' says Grant, 'Make sure you don't force me to release my grip otherwise who knows what will happen to your partner.'

I do as he says. He directs Amanda to put her hands behind her back. He orders her to cuff herself, all the while watching me. Then he tells me to place my mobile phone on the coffee table next to Amanda's. 'Okay, DS Rockwell come with us, you first. He waits until I'm level with him then he indicates by nodding his head that I'm to walk along the corridor. We get to a study to the left of the long hallway. He tells me to go inside. I hear the door being locked.

Amanda watches as Grant puts the batch of keys back in his pocket and waits for further instructions. She sees him put both the police phones in his pocket. He probably knows he can be tracked, she thinks, and suspects he'll toss them away somewhere during his escape.

'Out through the front door,' says Grant firmly, 'And no tricks.'

With hands cuffed behind her, Amanda moves cautiously. She can't risk a fall down the stone steps. The view when she can take a glimpse is spectacular. The city in the distance as well as the Sydney Harbour Bridge. This guy can live comfortably for the rest of his life. Why did he need to resort to violence? To murdering a so-called friend? Couldn't he just have let it go. Not only does he have wealth and a great career but also a beautiful partner in Fiona. Amanda is mystified by his apparent ego. To kill somebody for words spoken many years ago.

Downstairs, Grant pulls keys out of his pants pocket and presses a remote for the garage. Inside are three vehicles: a blue BMW, a white Lexus and a red Porsche 911. The pair walk inside. Grant chooses the white Lexus and pushes Amanda to the rear of the car. He opens the boot and forces Amanda inside. As the door shuts with a bang, Amanda tastes bile, a stomach reaction when she is stressed. She realises that Grant, despite his background and sophistication is capable of killing, and that her life is in danger.

Amanda hears the car roar off. She has no idea of his intentions. Amanda is not happy. Nor comfortable. Lying on her side, cuffed from behind, she feels every corner, braking and surge in acceleration the vehicle makes. As much as she tries to focus on the direction the powerful car takes, she cannot keep track of the corners, after the journey has gone more than fifteen minutes. Apart from trying to hold herself as still as possible to reduce the pain of being hog-tied, the change in direction has now occurred too often to provide any guide later, in the event she's alive to tell the tale.

The room I've been shut in has no windows so I can't escape by smashing the outside glass. I figure this room, an old-fashioned study with books aligned along rows of shelves which run along three walls from floor to ceiling, is impossible to break through without serious power tools. There's no point in speculating about it so I turn to the only wall which is different from the others, the one which has a door. The wall looks solid. Could it be oak or something? I have no idea as I'm no handyman. I can only distinguish between brick and wood and maybe plastic.

The roar of a vehicle outside alerts me to Amanda's plight. She's with that murderous bastard, and I'm stuck in here. My rage can't be exploited. I'll have to save it up for a future meeting.

I kick the door, but nothing happens except an uncomfortable thud to my foot. I straighten up, checking I haven't broken something. After a moment I realise I'm not permanently damaged. I look around. There's a desktop computer. I wonder if I can use it to alert someone although I suspect the programs are password protected. But I have to try. I sit in front of it and switch the tower on. Before I can examine further what is possible, the door opens.

Startled, I look up. It's not Grant, come to exact some vengeance. No, it's the lovely Fiona. Although I should be jumping up and down and rushing to the door, I can't help admiring her slim lines and long legs. She is dressed in something fashionable. I know because it looks fashionable and I've not seen anyone else wear the same clothes. 'Thank God,' I say. Although I'm not religious, I'm apt to use this term for good outcomes.

Fiona looks genuinely surprised. 'What are you doing here? At Grant's computer?'

I stand. 'Grant locked me in. He's taken my partner as a hostage.'

'Why?' Fiona asks.

'He's the murderer. Where would he have gone?'

'This doesn't make sense. Why would he have murdered Brent?'

I push past Fiona to search for my phone. 'Because Brent teased him at school for being gay.'

'Oh,' says Fiona following me.

'He's taken my phone. Can I borrow yours?' I ask, turning to face Fiona.

Fiona says, 'Sure.' She walks to where she dropped her handbag, rifles through it and finds the Samsung mobile phone. She hands it to me and frowns. 'Why would he kill for being teased decades ago?'

'We don't know. Is he gay?' I ask, knowing this is a delicate topic but I guess weirder things than two people who aren't straight living together have happened. Not something that's happened in my world, of course.

'He may be bi,' says Fiona. 'He does seem to mix with lots of guys. I thought he was simply a faithful man. Very unusual if you're handsome, I suspect.'

'Damn biologically impossible,' I say. What was she thinking – he's good looking, rich, has a fabulous job, is well mannered, monogamous and straight. Come on. 'Now I need to make a call. Can you describe the car he's driving?'

'I saw he took the Lexus.'

'Okay. Details please.'

After obtaining the information from Fiona, I call in and put out an alert on Grant Michaels and the vehicle he could be driving, I also advise that he is armed, has a police woman as a hostage and is dangerous. Then I turn back to Fiona. 'Where would he go?'

'I don't know,' she says, touching her blonde hair with a hand sporting immaculately polished red nails.

"Does he have a holiday house or a friend he would visit?'

Fiona takes a cigarette out of her bag and lights up. I can't say anything as it's her house, but I'd be surprised if Mr Perfect approved of her smoking. 'Nothing obvious comes to mind. You people would cover family but then he rarely goes to family.'

'Does he have means to get out of the country? Buddy with a yacht or a private plane?'

'No. I don't know him that well DS Rockwell.'

I'm stunned by this revelation. 'You live with the guy. I'd expect you'd know him better than anyone.'

'He's a very private person. And a bit secretive.'

'Really. Aren't you interested?'

'It suits me too. I have my secrets.'

'Are you gay too?'

Fiona laughs. 'Nothing like that.'

I didn't want to get into personal territory unless it related to Grant so I don't ask what her secrets are. 'I need to get going. You have my card so if you think of where Grant might be headed, please call. The longer he's a fugitive with a police officer as hostage, the worse it will get. Try his number first. I doubt he'll have kept his phone, but you never know.'

Fiona calls Grant's number, using the 'Speaker' function to allow me to listen. There is no response.

'Just as I thought,' I say. 'Thanks for your help.' As I'm about to exit, I turn around and ask, 'Did you have any idea that Grant killed Brent?'

'None whatsoever. How could I?'

'You were sharing a cabin with him. Did he just sneak out?'

'I don't know. I took a sleeping pill as I hadn't slept well so even if he left the cabin after we got there, I had no idea.'

I close the door and stride down the steps. I believe her. Her facial features betrayed nothing to suggest she was lying.

THIRTY-NINE

Amanda is terrified. She cannot work out how long they've travelled but it's feels like a long time. Is he going to run her into bushland and dispose of her? She doesn't want to think about it. She wants to remain positive. But she can't. Thoughts of impending death assails her mind. She's also in pain but her thoughts are causing more stress than the physical assault on her body from being trussed up like a hapless chicken.

Amanda stiffens. The car comes to a sudden halt. She hears loud noises, then identifies them as human shouts from outside but can't make out the words. Moments later the boot is opened, and she's so pleased to see Hank's face that she'll forgive him anything. He helps her out and, with a key, releases her sore wrists and arms. He gives her a hug and she's almost in tears with joy.

'Thank you so much,' says Amanda, 'I thought I was going to die.'

'Thank God you're unharmed. The helicopter squad found you after I got a lead from Fiona.'

Yes, we were lucky. Fiona had called me a few minutes after I'd left the Watsons Bay house to tell me one of Grant's friends had a holiday place on the Central Coast. And so, we punted on that as a possible destination and had all police stations north of Hornsby alerted. A helicopter was also despatched.

Now as I look at Amanda, I see she's still in shock. I call over a female constable and tell her to take Amanda to the nearest hospital to check out that's she's all right. I say to Amanda, 'Trudy will take you to a hospital. I want you to take a couple of days off. No argument. I'll catch up with you next Wednesday or Thursday if you're up to it.' I walk off, not waiting for a response.

On Wednesday, as I stroll into Headquarters, with coffee carton in hand, not thinking about anything in particular, I find Amanda waiting for me in my office. It's eight-thirty and Amanda is reading the Sydney Morning Herald.

'Hello,' she says.

'Hi, you seem very chipper so early in the morning.'

'I'm feeling good being alive. And the case has been solved which is a bonus.'

I sit down. 'Had I known you'd be in, I would have got you a coffee too.'

'Don't worry, I've already had one. What happens now? Do I get transferred back to Bondi?'

'Not exactly,' I say then sip some of my cappuccino. 'The case is still ongoing. Grant Michaels pleaded guilty to resisting arrest and kidnapping but not guilty to murder. He also said he acted like he did because he was afraid for his life. He said he was mentally unstable when we entered his house.'

'My God. Did anyone believe him?'

'That's his defence and he has retained some of the best counsel in the state. He's currently applying for bail and he'll probably get it, according to the prosecutor.'

'We have evidence, don't we, that he …' Amanda shifted in her seat.

'The phone recording won't stand up in court as the sound is so poor. And that's all the hard evidence we have.' I sit back and observe Amanda who looks so much better than when I helped her out of Michaels' boot. 'We need to build a case. Candice can confirm

Grant was teased years ago by Brent. We can also inform the court of his reaction when we mentioned what he was subjected to at school. But that's fairly thin.'

'What do you suggest we do?'

'We now know who killed Brent so we can focus on Grant Michaels. Find out everything about him. Interview school friends, teachers, work colleagues, family, current friends, Fiona. Do whatever it takes to build up a complete profile of this man.'

'Okay, who else is on the team?' Amanda crosses her legs.

'Alex, you and me. Are you feeling well now? You'll probably have nightmares for some time.'

'I feel fine except for the occasional bad memory when I'm in a confined area.'

I look her in the eyes. 'Let me know if you need help. You're seeing the police psychologist, aren't you?'

'Yes, once a week.' Amanda returns my gaze. 'Thanks again Hank for rescuing me the other day.'

I smile. 'My pleasure. I was worried about you and it's just as well other police officers were on the scene because I would have beat that sod to a pulp.'

Amanda sighs and puts her hand over mine. 'You care about me still,' she says. She rises from her chair and leaves the office without another word.

I was advised by a colleague that Grant Michaels was released on bail two days later. In the office now, leaning back, I sit and contemplate the situation. Has the world gone mad? But I've seen it before. Criminals who'd carried out the most ghastly crimes given a break through the system. Often, they were represented by expensive barristers who knew what arguments to put. It disgusts me but I cannot change the way the legal processes work. I use the internal telephone to invite Amanda into my office.

'Have you heard?' She asks, as she sits in front of me.

'Yes,' I say. 'What's been happening? Anything on Michaels?'

'Nothing significant, unfortunately. Found a sister he hasn't seen for years. Lives in country New South Wales. She said he was a shy lad growing up. Didn't like school much but always got good marks.'

'I see. Why haven't they been in touch? Did Michaels not like the sister?'

'I don't know. It was a telephone conversation.'

'Okay. Look, go visit her and see if you can establish any problems he had when he was young.'

Amanda crossed her suit trousered legs. 'What are you going to do? Interrogate Candy further?'

'No. I haven't seen Candice for weeks. She's overseas on business. I'm going to follow our friend to see what he gets up to.'

'He'll be on the lookout,' says Amanda.

'Yes, but I'm going to dress in such a way he won't suspect it's me.'

'Really. How's that, as a homeless person? You're nearly there now.' Amanda laughs.

'I'm not telling, smarty,' I say to move the topic on, to something else. "When you visit the sister, take somebody along.'

For the next few days and nights, I tail Grant Michaels. Nothing much happens. He's at home mainly. Occasionally, he goes to a café or a grocery store. At nights, he stays in. He can't work, as directed by the court, so he can't go into the office. And Fiona has taken flight, obviously not impressed that he's a killer. So, I wonder what's he up to. Is he plotting an escape, one without a passport or is he home reading, examining the internet or watching movies? The surveillance is boring, but I have a partner who does alternate shifts.

Then on Friday night, Michaels goes out. I wait until he's a few hundred metres up the road before I follow, lights out at first, and when he gets onto a main road, I switch them on. But now there is traffic, and I can follow at a distance. I nudge my partner awake.

'Some movement,' says John, 'that's better than sleeping in the car night after night.'

'Couldn't agree more,' I say. Fifteen minutes later Michaels parks his car near Taylor Square.

I get John to follow him on foot as Grant might recognise me if I walk after him. 'Text me when you reach his destination,' I say.

'Copy that,' says John. He gets out of the car then I move on to find a park in this densely packed part of town.

After I park, I walk about to stretch my legs. Being cooped up in a vehicle day and night, except for a few breaks, makes the job miserable. Although I should have assigned somebody to do this work instead of me, I wanted to nab this over-privileged sucker whenever I found he had transgressed bail restrictions. Already, he has moved out of the vicinity he'd been allowed by the judge. Once John returns, I intend to arrest him and lock him up for the night.

My phone alerts me to a text. John texts, 'Michaels is in a gay bar.'

I laugh to myself. Why the fuss? Michaels is entitled to lead this life. Nobody cares anymore. He killed Brent simply because he was called 'gay' during school days. Why did he bother? It suggests that the man, despite being successful and rich, is unhinged. But then during my time as a police officer, I've seen enough not to be surprised or shocked by any human behaviour.

I walk to where Michaels has parked his car. I text John to stay with Michaels and follow him when he leaves the bar. I lean on the hood of this expensive car realising that, on my salary, I'd never be able to afford something like this.

Finally, after time I didn't realise had lapsed, I see Michaels approaching. When he sees me, he appears startled, as though he's seen a ghost or men from Mars.

'What are you doing here?'

'I've come to make sure you haven't broken your bail conditions and, guess what, you have.'

Michaels pulls a pistol from his jacket pocket. 'You bastard.'

He points the gun at me, and I think this is the end. Where did he obtain this weapon? But worrying about it is futile now. I won't be able to do any more jobs. And I won't see Amanda or Candice again. I had a lot to live for but that's the risk this job entails. One never knows when it could go tits-up. I feel my insides protest and my heart pound. Should I stay here, frozen with fright or run and take the chance he might miss?

'Drop the weapon,' I hear. It's John. Thank God, he did as I asked.

Michaels turns but doesn't lower his gun. Before Michaels can shoot, John hits him in the chest twice. Michaels slumps to the ground. At first, I'm stuck in the spot, glad to be alive. I check that John is not hurt before I move to where Michaels lies. I test for a pulse on his neck and wrist to establish that Michaels is dead. He's gone, I say to John. It's over and we've saved the taxpayer a lot of money.

FORTY

'You were lucky,' says the Commander, a man with slicked back fair hair. He'd called me in to chat, as he put it.

'Absolutely,' I reply. 'I thought I was history, as they say.' Although I had been summoned for an informal discussion, I feel uncomfortable. This guy isn't someone who simply chats. He is a serious man.

'You know that John Redwood still needs to be investigated, despite your account of events?'

I know the protocol and I didn't expect Grant Michaels' shooting wouldn't be investigated. What I don't follow is why the Commander wants to rub it in. Doesn't he believe the report I'd prepared? 'Procedure, I know.'

'Just you and Redwood at the scene? No other witnesses?'

What was I going to say? The other witness was the man who died. 'No, sorry, there was nobody else present.'

'You realise this is a delicate matter, don't you?'

'Of course,' I say, wondering whether the Commander knew Michaels' father or was concerned with the publicity of an investment banker dying. After all, he wasn't some Western Suburbs' aboriginal or African refugee whom one could easily dismiss.

'As long as you're aware. I want you to take some time off. Recharge the batteries, so to speak, until the investigation is concluded. You'll be called in if needed to answer questions,' says the Commander patting his hair flat.

'Naturally,' I say. I stand and walk out of his office. When I re-enter my office, I run into Amanda who'd placed a note on my desk.

'I heard what happened,' she says. 'Are you okay?'

'Yes. I'm alive.'

'Have you been asked to get counselling?'

'It's been suggested,' I say, admiring Amanda's figure. Today she's wearing tight trousers and a white blouse.

'Are you going to comply?'

'I'll see,' I say, wondering why she's so interested. Does it take a near death experience for people to care?

'I left a note, saying I've been transferred back to Bondi. I hope we can get together sometime.'

'Sure. What about Saturday night?'

'As a friend, I mean. An old boyfriend has got in touch.'

'Oh,' I say, feeling deflated. But maybe this is for the best. Now I won't have to choose between Amanda and Candice. 'I hope it all goes well for you.'

'Thanks. Must go, bye.'

I watch as Amanda exits the room. I sigh then get some personal gear together before taking my break.

* * *

I'm at the airport. The place is heaving with people coming and going. I check Candice's flight details and wonder what is taking so long. Has she missed the flight or been held up at customs for bringing in illicit items or for having too much luggage? I'm not a patient man and this hanging about is making me grumpy. But I persevere. I don't have a job to go to so I can relax. I don't know whether Candice will be surprised to see me or not. I didn't communicate collecting her at the airport, so I hope it's a pleasant surprise.

After another coffee whilst standing at the exit barrier, examining the faces of thirty or more arriving passengers, I'm about to reconsider my strategy. Just as I'm about to walk away, I see her. Candice is pushing one small carry-on bag and pulling a suitcase. Both are on wheels. I move to the entrance and her face breaks into a happy smile. We embrace. I take the suitcase and let her roll the carry-on.

'You look terrific,' I say. I've missed her. She's looking radiant as though somebody has proposed marriage to her.

'Thank you,' she says, 'I didn't expect you to meet me. Aren't detectives always on the job?'

'It's a long story. I'll tell you over dinner tonight.'

'I have things to tell you too.'

I guide her to where I've parked my car and we drive, without much discussion, to her place. I help her in with her belongings and, before I can suggest going to the bedroom, she says she needs to rest. I'm disappointed as I thought she'd be keen to rekindle our romance. I leave her unpack and say I'll pick her up at seven in the evening.

At dinner, I'm about to tell her my story when a waiter interrupts us. She then jumps in to say she needs to inform me that she's met somebody who has proposed to her. Completely blind-sided by this news, I don't bother to tell her what's happened to me. The dinner floats by, the wine and whiskey keeping me numb. As I've had so much to drink, I get a cab and suggest she does the same.

In bed, by myself, I can't help feeling everything has gone wrong. Where once I had a choice between two beautiful and wonderful women, now I have nothing. No job, no love, no nothing. I close my eyes and drift off to sleep.

I wake to the sound of music. Opening my eyes, I look about, trying to figure out where the sound is coming from. I stand and peer out the window. It seems a car parked outside is generating the sound, or rather noise, when I decipher what is playing. As I'm naked, I can't really pop outside and complain. It's nearly seven thirty on a sunny morning so I decide to shower and start the day.

Then I remember the day before. The Brent Morton murder case may be done and I'm lucky to be alive, but I've lost two lovers in quick succession. It does beg the question about fate. Of course, I don't believe in such nonsense but someone or something somewhere is conspiring against me. But rather than dwell on this, I realise it's another day and I should be positive. Anything is still likely. Having a doomed love life is nothing new for me. Instead I should carry on with the next case.

The day goes slowly and uneventfully. I return to my place at seven o'clock in the evening, having stopped off to buy a few items for dinner. I'm not really in the mood to cook so opt for the easy way out by making a sandwich. Before I commence, I hear a sharp rap on the door. Who could it be? I'm not in the mood for company. After dinner, I was going to watch a violent action movie. This always makes me feel calmer. Odd, I know, but it works for me.

I open the door. There's nobody there. Is somebody playing a prank? Is it a disgruntled person seeking revenge? Although I should keep my gun with me at all times, it's a tedious way to live. About to shut the door, two figures come around the corner of the house and appear to be jubilant. I don't know what to do, I'm so shocked.

Later, as Amanda and Candice sit on a sofa facing me, I ask what's happening. All of us have a glass of red wine in front of us. We've spent a few minutes on small talk, asking about our health and activities of the day.

Amanda speaks first. 'Candy and I have been in touch. We both realise we're in love with you.'

'Oh,' I say, stunned by this revelation.

'Yes,' says Candice, 'and we know it must be difficult for you to choose. Are we right?'

'Absolutely. I've never been in love before then the two of you come into my life so close together. I mean so close in time…'

'We know what you mean,' says Amanda. 'We've also come up with a solution.'

I shift in my comfortable leather chair. On the one hand, it's great to see them but on the other hand, I wonder whether I will like the solution.

Candice continues. 'We're all grown-ups. We like each other. Why can't we all live together in harmony?'

'Splendid,' I say. 'How will this work?'

'We thought you'd come up with the perfect solution, without guidance,' says Amanda. 'You're intuitive. After all you figured Grant was the killer well before we had any evidence that he was guilty.'

'Yeah, but I'm not that intuitive about females. They confuse me,' I admit.

'Why don't we share a house, all of us and see how that goes,' says Candice.

I nearly have a coronary. I drink more wine. Am I in the midst of a dream? Will I wake to find that my life is as ordinary as always? But no, they're both still sitting in front of me. All I can do is nod.